A FALLEN KNIGHT

LAURENCIA HOFFMAN

Thank you!
for reading!
L.H.

CHBB Publishing

Published by CHBB Publishing
Cover Design by Seventhstar Art Services
Edited by Lily Luchesi at Partners in Crime Book Services

CONTENTS

For Timothée Chalamet, who sets fire to my imagination.

PLAYLIST

- Pompeii — E.S. Posthumus
- Astronomical — SVRCINA
- Before the Dawn — Evanescence
- Serenta Immortale — Trailerhead
- Island — SVRCINA
- Atonement (The Number 23 Soundtrack) — Harry Gregson Williams
- Song of Hal: Strings in B Minor (The King Soundtrack) — Nicholas Britell
- The Sun's Gone Dim And The Sky's Turned Black — Jóhann Jóhannsson
- Ballade in F# Minor: Trebuchets (The King Soundtrack) — Nicholas Britell
- So Cold — Ben Cocks ft. Nikisha Reyes-Pile
- Say Something — A Great Big World
- Missing — Evanescence
- Slow Movement (Romeo and Juliet Soundtrack) — Craig Armstrong
- Broken Crown — Mumford & Sons

CHAPTER 1

Robin Durand was having a difficult day. Three good men had been lost in battle. Although he did not know them well, every loss was meaningful. He felt he should have done more to prevent them.

He entered a dark tent, a place where soldiers came for relaxation. There were eateries, breweries, and comfortable couches where they could decompress from the day's — or week's — events. It all depended on the length of their mission.

It was empty during this late hour, save for a young boy seated at a far table.

Robin walked over to a common area where the Telebirds were situated. He caught the eye of the boy, who had a twinkle in his eye as he sauntered over.

"Robin, sir? I-I mean...Sir Robin?"

The boy couldn't have been more than eleven years old. His hair was dark and matted, likely from the mud the trainees were required to crawl through day after day.

"How may I help you, young man?"

"My name is Irwing. I wonder—" He paused to clear his throat. "Can you tell me what those are?"

"A Telebird?"

The item in question had the appearance of a horn that was large at the mouth, its shape becoming slenderer as it curved downward and attached to a wooden base. Each Telebird was decorated in a different combination of colors, and attached to a wooden base.

"They act as a communication device. If you speak near the horn, or directly into it, your voice will come through to the person at the end of another Telebird." Robin tapped one of the bases. "All you have to do is speak the name of the person you would like to reach, and if they are near any Telebird, yours will find theirs. It helps if you know the location of the intended person."

"And what if you speak into a Telebird's horn without the intention of locating a particular person?"

"In that case, you may wind up communicating with a stranger. The invention's purpose is to find a person for you to communicate with. It doesn't distinguish between people, or discriminate."

The boy's brow furrowed. "But how is that possible?"

"Magic, of course," he answered with a smile.

Brow raised, the boy looked over his shoulder before lowering his voice. "I thought magic was bad."

"I suppose that depends on your personal beliefs. Whether or not magic is outlawed goes on a kingdom by kingdom basis. Here in Daloran, it is perfectly legal. So," he gestured to one of the devices, "if you wish to contact anyone, they're here for you to use."

The boy seemed apprehensive and it was understandable. Many blamed magic for everything that went wrong in the kingdom. Robin was one of the few who blamed humans. He held mankind accountable for their actions. Magic was not the issue.

"Thank you, sir. I'll consider it."

Irwing offered a salute before vacating the common area.

Robin had no loved ones. There was no one for him to communicate with. As private as he was, as they *all* were, he wasn't too proud to admit he craved human interaction and needed to hear someone's voice.

He wasn't the only warrior who didn't have a place to call home, but the others occupied their time with prostitutes, drinks, and games. Robin had no interest in those things. He spent most of his time reading and learning various skills from others.

He was the only soldier in his unit, and perhaps in any unit, who could provide medical aid, sing anyone to sleep, play an instrument, and sew. On his days off, many men came to him for the stitching of their clothing.

Robin sighed softly as he sat next to the Telebird, staring at it for a good while and wondering if he should bother. If he did, there was no telling what kind of person would be on the other end.

He decided to risk it.

"Hello? Is anyone out there?"

To his surprise, he heard a woman's voice come through. "I thought I was the only one who couldn't sleep."

"My name is Robin Durand." He paused to consider how much to tell the stranger. "I reside in the kingdom of Daloran."

"My name is Arabella Renatus. I'm staying in Iros."

Robin looked over his shoulder to be certain he was alone. Conversing with anyone in Iros was forbidden, but if he would give the benefit of the doubt to any other stranger, that same courtesy should be extended to her.

"I've never been to Iros. What is it like there? I've heard that the palace was built entirely of crystals."

"Oh, yes. It is a city of crystals and the castle was built using a variety of them, although it was reinforced with marble and stone. It's beautiful and bright, sometimes too much for my liking. The crystals almost appear as diamonds to those who don't know any better, and I have no interest in such things." She paused. "Besides, the crystals are cold to the touch."

"It sounds breath taking to visit, though certainly not to live there. Daloran is cold, but for different reasons. We are surrounded by dirt, rock, and few resources. We rely on trades and shipments from nearby kingdoms, and our infamous boulders are the only things we have to offer."

"I think I would prefer it there, even if it is cold," she spoke in a wistful tone. "You sound young, Robin. How many years are you?"

"I'm old enough to serve in the army."

Swallowing hard, he shifted in his seat. Perhaps that had been the wrong thing to mention. Their kingdoms were at war. Some would say this interaction was treasonous, but Robin only thought of it as two people having a conversation. He would never give away any information that would be damning to the queen or her army.

All he wanted was a genuine friend; someone who was not obligated to tolerate him because their allegiance was the same. He wanted someone to like him for who he was.

"Well, that isn't saying much." He could hear the hesitancy in her voice. "From what I hear, your queen recruits her soldiers when they are children."

"Yes, that is true. We are taken from our families and train for years before being declared official soldiers. Queen Roanna demands perfection."

"I can imagine. Forgive me if I've offended you."

"No offense taken." Smiling to himself, he folded his arms. "However, I, being a gentleman, would never dream of asking your age."

The sound of her laughter was like music to his ears. "That has always been an issue, my not being a gentleman. I offer my sincerest apologies."

"Accepted, of course."

"I admire your spirit, Robin. I grow tired of seeing the same faces and hearing the same voices day after day. A new one would be most welcome."

It was rare to find another person who was just as lonely as he, and although he wouldn't wish it on anyone, it made him happy to know he wasn't alone.

He spoke with the other soldiers and they were friendly, but it was different. They didn't want to spend time with one another away from camp; too many reminders of the horrors they'd seen. They were only friends because they served together.

"Do you truly believe two strangers from opposing kingdoms can be friends?" he asked.

"Our countries are at war by no fault of ours. If you are willing to put our differences aside for the sake of a new friendship, then so am I."

"I look forward to our friendship and will embrace our differences." He wondered what Arabella looked like; if she was short or tall, if her hair was brown or blonde, how old she was. Since she had asked about his age, he assumed the possibility that she was older than him. "Will you tell me about yourself? I want to know everything."

He wasn't able to see her face, but he could hear the trepidation in her voice. That, and she paused before speaking.

"If I tell you everything now, you will tire of me and have no desire to speak to me after tonight."

"Oh, I doubt that."

Robin heard someone outside, and while he was sure the person was just going about their business, he didn't want anyone to overhear them. "Arabella, I should go. It sounds like people are stirring. Will I talk to you again?"

"Of course," she said. "Let's plan to check the Telebirds every night, if we're able. And if we're not, we'll find each other somehow. Have you ever used an enchanted falcon for communication purposes?"

"I can't say that I have."

"It's quite simple. Write a letter and tell the falcon the person you wish for them to deliver the letter to. Speak their name and the falcon will find them. Think of it as the physical version of a Telebird."

"That sounds perfect. I bid you goodnight."

Robin stepped away from the device knowing he wouldn't be able to sleep. How could he when he'd experienced the most refreshing conversation of his life?

He wanted to know more about her, what she was thinking, and what she thought of *him*. Telebirds were a marvelous invention, but it didn't replace seeing a person's face or reading their expressions.

THE OTHER SOLDIERS WERE TALKING OF THEIR PLANS FOR the future. Some of them were nearing the age of retirement. Robin listened intently, wondering what that would be like. It was no secret that most of Daloran's soldiers did not live to see retirement, and many of them preferred to die in battle.

"I'm going to spend my days in brothels and breweries, eating and drinking my way across the kingdom," one of them spoke with enthusiasm.

"I would like to travel," another mused. "I've never seen any of the other kingdoms in Terok."

"I want to have a family," a third stated quietly.

Robin's gaze was immediately glued to the man.

"The last time I was happy, I was with my family," he continued. "The joy on the faces of my parents any time we were all altogether, the love my siblings and I had for one another...I wish to experience that again." Head bowed, the soldier shook his head. "And I pray I will have daughters so they never have to fight in Queen Roanna's army."

The admission stunned the men into silence. They were not in the habit of sharing their feelings nor their true opinion of the queen's tactics.

"Those are treasonous words," the first mumbled.

The man who had bared all kept his gaze focused on the ground while he shrugged. Robin recognized the expression on his face; one of defeat. He'd seen it many times before.

"That is my dream too," he spoke up.

Each of their gazes turned to him. The man he'd addressed looked up with a nod and a small smile. A silent understanding. They were of the same mind, and though many may have agreed with them, they would never find their voice.

"Getting ahead of yourself, aren't you, *boy*?" the second man snapped. "You have many years of servitude before you're eligible for retirement."

It would be another ten to twenty years before he could consider it, depending on his physical fitness; never mind his emotional state.

He wasn't sure he had another twenty years left in him. Or even ten.

Young though he may be, the constant wars made him feel as if he'd lived several lifetimes, and was now an aging fool with nothing to show for it. He didn't want his entire life to pass him by without accomplishing anything worthwhile. His life could be summed up in one action; he killed people.

He fought in battles, moved from land to land to pursue whatever war he was ordered to.

Robin barely remembered his parents and his sister, but he thought about them more and more as time went on. And the more he thought of them, the more he wanted a family of his own.

He longed to have a place to call home. And he wanted friends, *true* friends that he could rely on for anything; friends he could confide in.

All fighting was tiresome, and it was equally exhausting to have nothing that was stable. Without the balance of a happy home life, only misery existed. The few possessions he had were on him at all times; his clothes and weapons. He had no pictures or letters from loved ones.

That wasn't the legacy he wanted to leave behind.

⚜

IT WOULD TAKE SEVERAL DAYS — PERHAPS WEEKS — TO reach their destination. If not for his talks with Arabella, the journey would have been a lonely one.

He had managed to find a vacant room on the ship and took the Telebird with him. Privacy had been a challenge before, and now there was even less of it. There weren't many quiet places on a ship crowded with soldiers.

"Do you often sail to other countries?" Arabella asked him.

"Only when it is my duty. We don't have the freedom to come and go where we choose, but I would like to be afforded that luxury."

"Freedom or the ability to travel?"

"Both."

"Be careful, Robin. You have referred to the soldiers of

your kingdom as though you are not one of them. That is dangerous."

He chuckled. "Are you concerned for my safety?"

"You know I am. What use are you to me without a head? I think you will earn your freedom someday."

"In truth, I wouldn't know what to do with it."

"What do you most enjoy when you're on leave? You can start there. I find nature to be my greatest comfort."

Another thing they had in common. "Nature is a beautiful thing. A gift. Perhaps one of the first things I will do when I return is take a walk in the woods." He paused to think for a moment. "I must tell you it cheers me to know someone is concerned for my well-being."

"Don't you have friends?"

"There is one man who I consider to be a true friend. His name is Trystan." He folded his arms. "He doesn't open up to anyone. Not even me. I don't want to be that way, closed off from the rest of humanity. I know that, for most, it is easier. But it's no way to live."

"Most of my friends are married with children. They care for me, but they don't understand me." A sigh could be heard through the Telebird. "Do *you* have anyone who understands you?"

Robin had to give that some thought. His only true friend was Trystan, and though he was certain Trystan would care if anything terrible befell him, he wasn't always certain the man cared about him as a *person*. Most of the time, Robin felt that Trystan was simply going through the motions. "I have companions, but none who care for me. I think it's more out of an obligation to our brotherhood. There is not a soul that truly understands me. Except...for you, I think."

There was a pause. "My dear Robin, you seem to understand me better than my closest friends. You are precious to me."

"As are you to me."

It was dark and everyone was piling into their bunks. Robin bid her farewell and then returned to his assigned room.

ROBIN CONSIDERED HIS HORSE, SHADOW, TO BE HIS TRUEST friend. He was a beautiful black stallion with an exceptionally long mane. Shadow had been with him for years. No matter what happened, if he fell, became wounded, or if he was miles away during a fight, Shadow would find him.

That was why he took it personally when someone insulted Shadow. They should have known better.

Robin was often teased for his boyish looks and scattered freckles. There were times when the other soldiers made jokes about his scars; one that interrupted his right eyebrow, and another that lined his left cheekbone. Insults directed at him could be tolerated, but Shadow was off-limits.

Simian, the man Robin was sitting on, found it difficult to breathe. Robin was fully dressed in his armor and Simian was not. "Get off me, you great oaf!"

"No." Robin examined his fingernails. "Not unless you take back what you said."

"It's a bloody horse!"

"He's *my* bloody horse. Take it back."

"Fine." Simian rolled his eyes. "Shadow does not look, nor does he *smell*, like a rotting carcass. Now get off me."

Satisfied, Robin got to his feet and helped Simian up. He chuckled, shaking his head as he walked over to Shadow and stroked his ears. "I hope you learned your lesson, Sym. We all know what rotting carcasses look *and* smell like, so how you could say such a thing about my Shadow is beyond me."

"Good lord," Simian grumbled. "You go loopy every time someone insults something that's dear to you."

"And is it unwarranted?"

"You overreact to everything. If I didn't know any better, I'd say you didn't like me."

"Perhaps if you stopped insulting me and my horse, we would get along better."

Simian was the teaser of the group. This was a typical interaction between them and Robin knew not to take it to heart. It was all in good fun and they needed some way to ease the tension.

Besides, it made the others laugh.

"You know better than to pick on Shadow," Willis, another soldier, said. "He's all Robin cares about."

Willis was the laugher. When he started to giggle, it took a while for him to stop, and his face always changed color.

"That's not true." A third soldier, named Derynk, gave a toothy grin. "I've heard him talking to someone in the common area several times this week. It seems he has a secret."

Robin pursed his lips, attempting to show as little emotion as possible. The more he cared, the more they would tease. "Yes, well...we all have secrets."

"So, what's yours then?" Willis asked. "Do you fancy other men?" He was biting his lip, trying to stop the inevitable fit of giggles.

"You would love that, wouldn't you, Will?"

"Of course I would, Curly-Locks. What man could resist you?" Finally, Will gave in and started to laugh.

With a roll of his eyes, Robin turned away from the group only to see their commander approaching them.

"Settle down, men," Jacob said. "I bring news."

Robin corrected his posture as he faced his superior, as did they all. "What news?"

He watched as the older man shifted his weight from one leg to the other. "We have received news that the army of Iros intends to head for Daloran, so we must beat them to it by invading their land. Iros' army has strength in numbers, but they don't have our spirit. This attempt at a sneak attack changes nothing but the direction in which we'll strike."

Robin was eager to return to his bunk as their commander continued a familiar message. It was the same speech they heard over and over. They never knew what danger awaited them. Although they had been trained to prepare for the unexpected, he couldn't help but wonder how either side would win this war when it was so unorganized.

"Robin, would you mind staying a moment?"

He waited for the others to vacate the premises before nodding. "What is it, sir?"

"My injury has rendered me incapable of participating in combat."

"Yes, sir. I'm aware."

Gaze downcast, Jacob cleared his throat. "When Queen Roanna ordered me to be removed from my post, I thought my career was over. I was...overwhelmed when you and the other men requested my involvement at camp, regardless of my ability to fight."

"You're a good man, Jacob. Men like you are difficult to come by."

While he was no expert in emotions, it appeared as though his superior was embarrassed. Their request to keep him there may have done wonders for their morale, but not much for Jacob's pride, it seemed.

"I'm not well enough to lead the charge."

Robin nodded slowly. "It's alright, sir. I can do it."

"I know it's unfair of me to ask."

"No, it isn't. We requested you remain at your post

knowing full well that you wouldn't be able to lead us into battle."

Jacob raised his chin, looking as though a weight had been lifted off his shoulders. "Thank you. I thought I'd lost my worth."

He furrowed his brow. "Sir, your worth extends far beyond your ability to wield a sword."

This brought tears to the older man's eyes. "That's very kind of you to say."

"Has anyone..." Glancing around to ensure that no one was paying attention to them, he then took a step closer. "Has anyone ever told you that before?"

Jacob shook his head.

It hadn't occurred to him that the Captain might be in need of a kind word. He assumed Jacob had support, perhaps from family at home or friends nearby. Now he was sorry he hadn't said something sooner.

"There is no shame in this." Robin placed a hand on his shoulder. "There's a whole world out there yet to explore. If this injury prompts an early retirement, I envy you. And you've earned it."

With a chuckle, Jacob shook his head. "You're different from the other soldiers. In all my years of service, no other man has spoken openly of wanting a life outside of the battlefield."

He shrugged. "I suppose it's because they don't believe there *is* a life outside of the battlefield. We are taught to serve and protect at an early age, and to think of nothing else."

"Is that what you believe?"

Robin licked his lips anxiously, fearing anything he said might be taken as treason. "No. I think there is more to life than death. There has to be. Nonetheless, I will defend the crown with my life."

Before he opened his mouth again and gave too honest of

an answer, he went straight to his bunk and pulled out a piece of paper, ink, and a quill. Robin couldn't wait for the common area to be unoccupied to contact her. If they were unable to communicate through the Telebirds, they had agreed that using letters was the best alternative.

Arabella,

I cannot say much, only that I have recently acquired more responsibility and I am anxious.

THE FACT THAT HE HAD TO REMIND HIMSELF NOT TO GIVE away their position frightened him. He was becoming too comfortable with her; it was easy to forget that she was from the land of the enemy.

After rolling up the parchment, he placed it in the mouth of an enchanted falcon, who flew away to Arabella's whereabouts.

If they were caught, they could be charged with treason. That was why it was imperative to keep their discussions short through letters. Their focus was on each other. While he couldn't speak for Arabella, it never crossed his mind to attempt to gain information from her in order to use it for Daloran's gain.

Robin had served in the army of Daloran his entire life and always considered himself to be a loyal person. Now, his view of the world was changing.

The enemy was not simply their enemy. They were people too. They had lives, hopes, and dreams; no different than anyone in Daloran.

Why should he view them as evil? He understood that it was necessary to think of them as such in order to be able to strike them down when needed, but they were no longer face-less. He was becoming awakened to the hypocrisy of war.

All he could do was wait. Wait for everything. Wait for

orders, wait for battle, and wait for Arabella's reply. He soon dozed off, but woke to what he had been hoping for.

A letter.

ROBIN,

I hope that your journey will be a safe one. We have corresponded far too often to never meet in person. Be careful.

IT BROUGHT A SMILE TO HIS FACE THAT SHE WAS WORRIED; it meant she cared. Never in his wildest dreams had he thought that something like this would happen to him.

He had never planned to fall in love or have a family, only to fight and die for his country. Now he found himself caring for a woman he had never met. He could only hope her feelings mirrored his own, at least, to some extent.

Robin quickly scribbled his reply and gave it to the falcon.

DEAR ARABELLA,

Believe me, if I stay alive for nothing else, it will be to see your face.

IT WAS DAYS LIKE THESE ROBIN LOOKED FORWARD TO — when he and Arabella had time to write back and forth to each other for an extended period of time.

He wondered where in Iros she was located. She could have been in any part of the country, though, perhaps, they could meet at the border between kingdoms.

He was pulled from his thoughts as the falcon returned with another letter, and this time it carried something else in its beak as well; a silver-banded ring with a Moonstone in the center.

ROBIN,

Wear this as a token of my affection. It belonged to my grand-mother. May it bring you luck as you navigate your new responsi-bilities.

HE IMMEDIATELY PLACED THE RING ON HIS PINKY, EAGER to be able to touch something that belonged to her. It made the distance between them seem a little less now. It gave him hope for a new life. And a future.

ARABELLA,

This gives me all the motivation I need to return home. I will carry it with me always.

ROBIN KNEW THAT WOULD HAVE TO BE THE LAST LETTER OF the night, lest they risk discovery.

CHAPTER 2

Feeling that he may be in for a sleepless night, he took out Arabella's letters, which were kept in a box tucked under his bed.

"What are those?"

Robin was relieved to look over and see Willis. He knew Will wouldn't tease him. "They're letters."

"I can see that. Who are they from?"

"If you must know, they're from a woman."

"Oh!" Willis laughed. "Well, who is she?"

Licking his lips anxiously, he pondered his answer. He had never asked Arabella her occupation. They had discussed far more important matters. "I don't know."

"Well, what does she look like?"

"She's...beautiful."

Willis scrunched his nose as he seemed to realize that Robin didn't know how to answer his question. "Have you met her?"

"Not yet, but soon."

He threw a pillow toward Robin's face, which he dodged easily. "What on earth are you thinking?"

"I don't know what you mean. She's wonderful."

"I mean that she could be an ugly, old hag," Willis said with a scoff.

"That doesn't matter to me."

He shook his head. "You truly are a mysterious man, Robin. One of a kind."

❧

AFTER TWO DAYS OF PACKING AND PREPARATION, THE SHIP finally set sail.

All Daloranians felt a sense of pride when leaving the docks for the Perfidious Sea. The waters were treacherous, filled with the infamous boulders their kingdom was known for. Only their people could navigate the sea. Many an enemy had perished on the rocks, although a few managed to find other ways to the land.

The men cheered upon entry to the Boundless Ocean; another successful ship launch.

Hours after setting sail, Robin remained on the deck. He couldn't stand to be cooped up in his cabin and needed the fresh air.

He walked toward the railing to calm his nerves and watched the ripples of the water as the ship moved through it. Quiet moments were rare and he appreciated each one.

This moment was different because it was the first time he wished someone else was beside him. He wanted Arabella to see how clear the water was and how the sun looked as it set; reflecting light on the Boundless Ocean.

He wondered if she had ever left her homeland. Had she sailed before? He hoped they could experience it together.

A tall man with brown hair and streaks of silver stood beside him and gazed into the water.

"Good evening, Trystan."

The man nodded in response. Robin was known as being someone who liked to keep to himself, but Trystan took that to the extreme. His brooding and stoic nature did little to dampen Robin's high opinion of him. They had similar experiences and that would solidify their bond forever.

Robin didn't mind Trystan's silence; he could do enough talking for the both of them. "You need a haircut, my friend."

Trystan chuckled and shook his head. "Never in your wildest dreams."

The older man's hair shielded his eyes and closed him off from the rest of the world. His face was as rough as most men who had seen the horrors of war. It was an appearance that kept others at a distance.

People didn't understand his friend as he did, nor did they have patience with him.

"Who is this woman I've been hearing about?"

Robin opened his mouth and then closed it again. He hadn't meant for him to hear it from the others. While he hadn't intended for *anyone* to discover that he had feelings for someone, it had only been a matter of time before they noticed a change in him.

"There's something about her...she's unlike any other woman I've ever met."

"Count yourself lucky then."

Robin never spoke to Trystan about family. He didn't know if his friend wanted one or if he thought about it as often as Robin did. There were some things they simply didn't discuss. Although they were the closest thing to a best friend that either of them had, there were a great deal of subjects they refused to broach.

"Should I ask her if she has a sister?"

"No." Trystan looked at him with a hint of a smile, though one never appeared. "I can't trust your taste in women, not now. You have feelings for someone you've never met. I still want a woman who's pleasing to the eye."

"I don't care what she looks like." He gave a sure nod. "She has the voice of an angel. It's soothing to me. It...sounds like home."

"I'm happy for you." Trystan placed his hand on his friend's shoulder. "Slightly envious, but happy."

"Don't be happy for me yet; after all, I still don't know what she looks like," he quipped.

THEY HAD BEEN INFORMED THEY WOULD BE DOCKING AT the Half-Point for the day. If he had a favorite location, it would be this. The Half-Points were always full of life. It was where friends safely reunited no matter where they'd come from, where people from all across Terok gathered.

With Trystan by his side, they walked past bustling streets, gaze wandering from various booths — vendors selling food, clothing, and other supplies.

"Tell me again why you enjoy the Half-Points so much," Trystan grumbled.

"Because they are under no royal jurisdiction."

"I say that makes them dangerous."

"Nothing bad happens here, my friend. It's neutral ground for all people."

"Just because nothing bad has happened yet doesn't mean it never will."

Stopping near a vendor selling silk, Robin smiled and folded his arms. His gaze was focused on two young women, not that anyone could tell their identities by the backs of their heads, but he would recognize their voices anywhere.

Trystan nudged him. "Are those the princesses of Daloran?"

"Yes," he said, though nodded for further confirmation. "I'm glad they're here. It means they're safe."

"For now." He shook his head. "Only *you* could befriend the royal family."

"*They* befriended *me*; I had no say in the matter."

"Which one is which?"

"You mean you've never met them?"

Trystan shook his head, looking entirely uninterested. Robin knew better than to introduce them. First, he gestured to the one slightly taller. He wouldn't be able to see from that angle, but she had dark hair and eyes to match. "That is Primrose. She's wise beyond her years. A queen in the making." Then he nodded to the other whose hair was a lighter shade of brown, and eyes, unseen, were hazel. "That is Bryony. She's a free spirit, quite sweet. Though, I suppose she *can* be, considering she's not in line for the throne. She has more freedom than her sister."

"Bryony will never have to think of taking the throne as long as we complete our mission," Trystan spoke with confidence. "Her mother and sister will live long and happy lives if we have anything to say about it. They deserve that much after the loss of their father."

"You know, you're not as terrible as you would have people believe." Turning to his friend, he raised his brow. "You should try talking to people. You might enjoy it. Smile every once in a while. You have frown lines."

"I'll talk to people when I'm dead."

"Trystan, you won't be talking to anyone when you're dead."

"Good, just the way I like it."

As the princesses turned around, Trystan walked in the opposite direction.

"Robin!" Bryony squealed.

"Good day, your Highnesses." He gave them both a hug and then took a step back. "How are you?"

"We're fine," Primrose said with a laugh. "But if I do recall, we've told you to call us by our first names!"

"I know, I know. It just seems so...informal."

"It's supposed to be, you silly goose. You're our friend."

"I am your humble servant, first and foremost."

"We know better than to try and change your mind. So stubborn." Bry clicked her tongue. "So how is our favorite knight? Do you have anything new to share?"

"As a matter of fact, I do." Robin hadn't told them about Arabella. He knew how strange it might seem to some that he was developing feelings for someone he had yet to meet. And Robin hadn't yet decided just how much he would speak of Arabella. He had no doubt that she was not a danger to their kingdom, but others wouldn't be so quick to trust her.

"What is it?" Prim asked.

"Well, there's a woman..."

"I knew it!" Bry squealed and hugged him. "Our Robin has finally met someone!"

"Don't get too excited." He chuckled. "We don't know each other well...yet." That wasn't true. Robin felt as though he had known her all his life. Perhaps they had known each other before, in a life before this one. But he had to be careful not to give away her background.

Prim placed her hands on her hips. "When do we get to meet her?"

"After I do," he answered hesitantly.

Bry's smile brightened and she clapped with enthusiasm. "Oh, Robin! You haven't even seen each other's faces? That's so romantic!"

"Let's not get ahead of ourselves." His cheeks were flushed. "We're only friends." That wasn't true either. Lying was becoming second nature to him.

"For now," Prim said teasingly.

Robin heard Jacob rounding up the other men. He sighed softly. It was always bittersweet to say goodbye to the princesses. He was happy to have seen them and disappointed to leave.

"Be safe, your Highnesses. And if you need anything, don't hesitate to write." He gave them each a long hug, and then stepped back with a smile. "I'll see you soon."

"Goodbye, Robin," Bry said. "Don't forget us while you're away!"

"And for goodness' sake, be careful," Prim added.

Robin settled into his bunk. He had to take advantage of the emptiness of his room and speak to Arabella while he could. He sat with the Telebird and waited for her to answer. It was always a relief to hear her voice. She was a welcome change to his current surroundings.

"The men are quiet but restless. I'm so thankful I have someone to talk to. I don't know how the others manage."

"You mean to say that I am a comfort to you?"

"Yes. A great one, at that."

"As are you to me."

He furrowed his brow. Something was different; her tone was deeper. It held a waver he'd never heard before, something mirroring sadness. "How are you fairing, Arabella? Are you well?"

There was a pause. "We're going into combat."

"Combat?" He looked over his shoulder to be certain he was alone. There was no creaking of the floorboard or the shuffling of boots, so he felt it was safe to continue. "What do you mean by that?"

Another pause. This time, it wasn't followed by a verbal

answer, but the sound of a sob.

"Arabella?" Licking his lips anxiously, he waited with baited breath. "Ari...*please*. Say something."

"You know that I live in Iros, but I've been hesitant to tell you the whole truth."

"And that is?"

"That I *fight* for Iros."

His stomaching was churning as hands gripped his knees. "You're a soldier in the Iros army?"

"N-not exactly." A sniffle could be heard. "I am serving in the League of the Satari."

"The Satari?" He furrowed his brow. "I've heard of them, but I thought they were a myth."

"Not a myth. What do you know?"

"That they're an organization of assassins." His fingers clutched his knees so tightly his knuckles turned white. "I imagine the league must be quite secretive. Are you putting yourself at risk by telling me this?"

"Knowing who we are is not an issue. As long as no one is aware of our mission while we are in the throes of it, we don't mind being known or seen. Our founder, General Marla Satari, has nothing to hide."

"An assassin," he hissed. "How could I have been so foolish to think you cared for me?"

"I do!"

Robin clenched his jaw while listening to the flood of emotion from the Telebird. Arabella was hysterical and trying to speak through her sobs. He closed the door to his cabin and then stood near the device.

He wanted to smash it to smithereens. Or, better yet, cast it into the sea. Speaking to a civilian may not have been considered a betrayal, but speaking to a member of any part of the enemy's army would surely cost him the head upon his shoulders.

As he took a deep breath and sat on the edge of his bed, he reminded himself, if she was fighting on Iros, then she was committing treason against her kingdom as well. If she was willing to cross the same line, and confess her truth, she must be invested in their correspondence.

Breath shaky, he closed his eyes. "Do you understand that I love you?"

All went quiet. There was an even longer pause and it sounded as if she was trying to steady her breathing. "You are not alone in your sentiments."

Tears welled up in his eyes as soon as he opened them. "What are we going to do?"

"I don't know. I was hoping you might think of a solution. All I know is that I love you."

Those three words made his heart soar and sink in fluctuation, making his heartbeat erratic. It was the very thing he'd been longing to hear his entire life. Why had fate been so cruel? A lifetime of torment and isolation hadn't been enough. He was now doomed to love a woman he could never be with openly.

It would mean death for both of them.

"Why did you continue to speak to me when you knew my position?" he spoke in a wavering voice.

"Like you, I was lonely. I was desperately searching for a connection. Something to take me away from the turmoil in my day-to-day life." Her voice broke. "I never meant to fall in love. I didn't want to. But I couldn't deny the relief I felt when hearing your voice. You've brought me such comfort, even from so far away, and I've often imagined how much that feeling would surely grow if we were to be in each other's presence."

All of him loved her, most of him believed her, but there was a small part that was afraid to trust her. It seemed they had felt the same way and had the same dreams.

Refusing her affections could cost him the only true love he'd ever known, and accepting them could mean ruin for the kingdom he swore to serve.

His own life mattered not. It was the innocent lives he feared for.

If Arabella became a casualty, whether she was lying about her feelings for him or not, it would kill him.

Robin glanced to the door, again listening for any sign of company. When there was none, he cleared his throat. "We must be very careful from here on out. More so than we have been before. I will be put to death if they suspect treason. I'm sure the same is true for you."

"It is." Emotion was still present in her voice, though it had lessened. "The only crime we've committed is falling for someone across enemy lines. Not once have we spoken of our plans or positions. I know nothing of your station or your army's movement and you know nothing of Iros'."

He heaved a sigh. "That won't stop either side from assigning blame. I think we are both aware of the temperament of our rulers."

"I dare say King Rydon would be more tolerant of my actions than Queen Roanna would be of yours. Are you certain this is what you want?"

The pace of his heartbeat quickened. He knew there was a possibility that they would never meet — either of them could die in battle, and he would be considered a traitor if they were ever caught.

All that aside, he *had* to meet the woman who changed his life. After so many years of burying his emotions and being taught to pretend as though they didn't exist, he finally felt comfortable expressing his feelings.

Saving lives — and taking them — was the only life he'd ever known. He'd gone from one war to the next with few breaks in between. Although he'd wanted it to end, he had never thought it would be possible for him to have a life beyond fighting.

He kept people at a distance because any moment could be his last, and he didn't see the point of building relationships only to be taken away from them.

Arabella had changed his beliefs. Now he knew that it was better to experience something, and lose it, than to never have experienced it at all.

"I regret nothing. You are the only peace I've ever known. Please tell me our conversations have not been for nothing. You must return. I need to see your face, to hold you..."

"I don't know what's going to happen, Robin." She was back to choking on sobs. "All I know is that, for the first time in my life, I have something to lose. I'm afraid."

Tears formed in his eyes at the admission. "You must have faith. Believe in yourself...as I believe in you."

⚜

THE DAYS WERE BLURRING. HE'D STOPPED COUNTING HOW long it had been since he and Ari last spoke. If he dwelled on it for too long, he would become fearful that her assurance of love had been a lie and she was informing the leaders of Iros about the whereabouts of Daloran's army.

Those thoughts faded quickly when he reminded himself that he and Arabella hadn't discussed such matters, though it did little to calm his nerves.

He wandered around the ship until he came to Trystan's room — unlike most others, his bunk was private.

"Any nightmares tonight, old friend?"

"Don't know yet," he answered with a shrug. "Can't sleep."

"Try sleeping with a room full of snoring men."

"Well, when you start having violent night terrors, you'll get your own cabin."

Folding his arms, Robin stood against the wall. "What do you think about this battle? How many will be lost?"

Trystan stood from his bed. "Are you anxious?"

"A little."

His brow furrowed. "I've never known you to be anxious about a fight. What's changed?"

Robin didn't have to answer that question. It only took Trystan a moment to realize he already knew the answer.

"Ah...it's that woman you've been corresponding with, isn't it?" He studied Robin's face and then grumbled, "You can't lose your focus. That's not good for anyone."

It wasn't that he lacked confidence in his abilities. There was always a chance they wouldn't return, but this was the first time he cared. "I want to make it home safely. It's not only me I have to worry about now. Someone is waiting for me."

"All you can do is fight without mercy and stay alive."

"I suppose you're right."

"I'm always right." Trystan chuckled, a truly rare occurrence. "Don't worry your pretty head. I'll watch over you and make sure you get to meet your woman, Curly-Locks."

Robin smiled and shook his head. He did feel safer knowing Trystan would fight alongside him. They always watched out for one another. "Thank you, my friend."

Dipping his chin, his gaze focused on his boots. He knew Trystan would not be so accommodating if he'd been aware of Arabella's alignment with the enemy.

IT SEEMED LIKE MONTHS BEFORE THEY REACHED LAND. Robin knew Arabella must have been as busy as he was because he hadn't heard from her.

Many of the men stood on deck to gaze upon the glittering waters of the Crystal Sea. Just as Daloran was known for their rocks, Iros was known for their crystals. Many colors of stone sparkled at the bottom of the clear water. They dared not anchor too close to shore, afraid the sharp edges may damage their ship.

Fear ran rampant among the men. Fighting on the enemy's territory was not ideal, but it was unavoidable. They had to strike before Iros put forth their plan to sail for Daloran.

After helping the other soldiers settle into their new camp, he walked toward Jacob's tent.

He announced himself before walking inside and furrowed his brow when he saw Jacob was lying down. "Forgive me, Captain. I didn't think you would be resting so late in the afternoon."

"It's alright." He sighed before sitting up. "What can I do for you?"

"I wanted to make sure that you were alright."

He was quiet for a moment, gaze wandering over the curly-haired brunet. "Was it unfair of me to ask you to lead the charge?"

"No, sir. It's an honor."

A look of relief washed over his commander's face. "You know I wouldn't have asked if it wasn't absolutely necessary."

"I do know that."

Jacob looked up at him, though he didn't move from the bed. "I'm dying, Robin."

Unprofessional as it may be, he couldn't hide his pained expression. His face scrunched momentarily before he could correct it. "I'm sorry, sir. I had no idea."

"I've accepted my fate. Though I have so many regrets..." His voice broke as he shook his head. "I have no one to carry on my family name. No wife, no children. No legacy to speak of."

He dipped his chin. That was the life he was trying to escape. A *lonely* one. "I can't imagine."

"I hope you never have to." Jacob grunted while lying back in the bed and adjusting his legs. "Do you have someone you care for?"

Robin swallowed hard. Bringing up Arabella seemed like a betrayal in itself. "Yes, sir. I do. I've been writing to a woman."

"Good." Jacob nodded. "Don't take her for granted. If you love her and she loves you, don't waste another second being apart. Life is too short."

"I won't waste it. I promise you. And, if I may..."

He gestured for Robin to continue.

"*We* are your legacy, sir. Your memory will live on in every person you've ever known, every soldier who is alive because of your leadership."

The older male was brought to tears. And then he whispered, "Thank you."

Robin went back to his own tent with a heavy heart. He thought it best not to spread the information. It was Jacob's choice to divulge such news.

It was so late in the evening most of the soldiers had gone straight to sleep after getting settled. A letter would have done wonders for his uneasy stomach. Alas, there were none. His talk with the Captain weighed on his mind as he drifted off to sleep.

He awoke to screams in the middle of the night. They were familiar sounds; he had memorized them all in battle. One of his men was in trouble.

Robin sprung out of bed with his sword in hand and followed the noise, but he arrived too late.

Two men were holding back a stranger. Willis was on the ground, covered in blood from chest to navel.

Robin knelt beside him, his eyes unbelieving of what they

saw. The man had been practically disemboweled. He would expect to see such a sight on the battlefield, not within the safety of their own camp. "What happened?"

"I was walking the grounds," Willis said hoarsely, "And I caught him trying to sneak into Jacob's t-tent, so I followed him..."

Robin glanced at the assassin. The man's eyes appeared black; they were the angriest he had ever seen. To his left stood Simian and Derynk, who shook their heads; confirmation that their Captain was dead.

Willis, oblivious to their knowledge, was staring at him expectantly. "Is Jacob alright?"

"He's fine," Robin lied. "You saved his life." He saw no reason to tell his friend that his sacrifice was in vain.

Willis took his last breath with Robin gripping his hand.

His jaw clenched as he peered into lifeless hazel eyes. He was partly to blame for the incident. Robin should have trusted his gut; that unsettling feeling he'd fallen asleep with. He should have kept watch instead of succumbing to rest.

He stood and faced the assassin. The man looked rather pleased with himself, a smug smirk donning his features.

"I was sent by my King to give a message to your leader," he said with a sneer. "But it seems you have no Captain to speak of."

As soon as the stranger grinned, Robin lifted his sword and buried it in the man's mouth. To his pleasure, the assassin did not die instantly. His eyes were wide, mouth full of steel and blood streaming from his lips.

"I would tell you to give your King my reply, but it seems you have no mouth to speak of."

Withdrawing his sword, he delivered a swift slice to the man's face before the body crumpled to the ground, the assassin's jaw landing near the mutilated head.

CHAPTER 3

The men were looking to him for answers and he had none to give. The assassin hadn't been identified. Should he have left the man alive to hear King Rydon's message? The ruler had to know their whereabouts in order to send a killer in the first place, so what did that mean for their plan of attack? The element of surprise was gone. Now, they waited with baited breath.

A pit had settled deep within his stomach over the last several days, for each one that passed by was another day Arabella hadn't contacted him, and another day that he suspected her being responsible for the assassin.

After all, she worked with a league of them. He hadn't given her their location, but that didn't mean she hadn't discovered it somehow.

What if she was corresponding with someone else in their battalion who had been all too willing to reveal their battle plans?

How could King Rydon know the exact location to send the assassin? They could have arrived on any side of the kingdom.

However the information had found the King was of little importance now. In a way, they were at King Rydon's mercy. The battle would play out when and how *he* saw fit. Queen Roanna's soldiers were at a disadvantage.

As acting Captain, it was his duty to decide how best to move forward. Retreat was not an option; the Queen would never accept that. Robin wanted to minimize the loss of life if at all possible.

He heard someone clearing their throat outside of his tent.

"Who is it?"

"I-it's Irwing, s-sir."

Irwing. One of the youngest soldiers in the unit, though he was not alone. The others called them soldiers but Robin thought of them as they were — children.

"Come in, Irwing."

The boy stepped inside the tent. He was shaking from head to toe. "I s-saw what happened to the Captain. And to Willis."

He remembered the first horrors he'd been subjected to as a child. Although soldiers were supposed to become numb to the violence, he had never become desensitized.

"I'm sorry you had to see that. What's on your mind, young man?"

"I'm afraid," he squeaked. There was sweat on his brow and tears in his eyes. "They were skilled fighters and...look what happened to them."

"I see." With a smile that he tried to pass off as reassuring, he motioned for the boy to come closer. "I'm just as fearful as you."

Irwing's gaze wandered over him. "You don't look afraid, sir."

"I've had years to learn how to disguise how I truly feel.

Here." Robin took Irwing's hand and pressed it to his neck. "Do you feel my pulse?"

His eyes widened as he nodded. "It's racing, sir."

"Precisely. You see, I'm still afraid, even after all these years. I was younger than you when I was recruited. It takes practice, but you'll get better at hiding your fear. There's nothing wrong with being afraid, Irwing. The only trouble is that it affects how you fight. You need steady hands to wield a sword and a clear mind to strike true."

"I understand, sir."

"Take deep breaths. Think of something that makes you feel calm. For me, it's water. I feel freest sailing the Boundless Ocean and varying seas, to be more precise. What is it for you?"

"Um...fields of wheat. They remind me of my family's farm."

"Very good, Irwing." Robin smiled and patted the boy's arm. "How do you feel now?"

"Still afraid, but..." He held out his hands to show that the shaking had lessened. "My hands are steadier."

"Well done, lad. You're a fast learner."

"Thank you, sir."

Biting the inside of his cheek, Robin gazed at the table near the side of the tent. There was a map and figurines scattered across it. He had gone over several options for their plan of attack. No matter how much he willed for every soldier to return home, it wasn't possible. There were always losses.

Now that he was the temporary commander, he couldn't justify sending children to their deaths.

"Irwing, how many friends do you have? How many soldiers of your age are there?"

"There are twelve of us, sir."

"That's precisely the number I need." Getting to his feet,

he placed a hand on the boy's shoulder. "I wish for you and your friends to remain at camp during the battle. Should things go awry, it will be your duty to destroy all of our battle plans. Before we leave, I will ensure that all plans and correspondence with the Queen and her advisors will be gathered in my tent. If we lose, someone will be sent to camp to warn those remaining here, and your assignment will be to set my tent ablaze. The enemy cannot get their hands on those plans. Do you understand?"

"Yes, sir. If the worst should happen, what will we do after we burn the contents of your tent?"

"You will go back to the ship with all remaining soldiers and instruct them to set sail."

"You would have us leave you behind, sir?" he asked breathlessly.

"If the worst should happen, you will have no other choice."

THE HOUR WAS LATE AND HE WAS RUNNING OUT OF TIME TO say goodbye. Robin knew that every time he engaged in battle, there was a chance that he may not return. This time, there was someone worth bidding farewell.

He waited until there was no sign of any soldier awake and then trudged to the tent serving as the common area. The debate in his mind was whether or not to question Arabella's intent or to give her the benefit of the doubt.

One part of him knew nothing but love for the woman he'd never laid eyes on, while the other grew ever suspicious.

Still, there was no doubt in his mind that, if this night would be his last alive, she was the one person he wished to speak to.

Swallowing his pride, Robin stood near one of the

Telebirds, cleared his throat, and then spoke her name clearly.

"Thank the stars you're alive!"

Her voice was as soothing as ever. "Was there any doubt?"

"I want you to know I had no knowledge of the assassin being sent. When I heard the news, and that there had been casualties within your camp...they said the Captain had been killed. You had told me that you were taking on more responsibility."

"And you assumed that I was the Captain. You thought I was dead?"

"Yes. That's why I was hesitant to use the Telebird or a falcon." He could hear sniffling. "Not knowing gave me hope. I couldn't bear it if I lost you. You are the sun in my sky."

"As are you to me."

"Without your light, my world would grow cold and dark. I don't want to know what life is like without you."

Shaking his head, he heaved a sigh. It was no use. He could deny his feelings for her and pretend that he could think objectively, but he'd be living another lie. "I love you, Arabella. Beyond all sense or reason...I do."

"I know that you are soon to fight. The League of the Satari will not be joining in this battle, so there's no chance of us fighting against each other."

"That is a relief. But I must admit I'm still at a loss for what to do."

"Come back to me. Live through this battle." Her voice wavered and he wished he could be there to comfort her. "The rest can wait, my love. There will be time to make decisions about our future."

"And you still want that? A life together?"

"More than anything."

If they didn't meet, this was all for nothing. It may not reveal her intentions, but at least he would be able to read her expressions. "Will you be near the battlefield even if you are not partaking in the fight?"

"Yes, I'll be close by."

"Then perhaps we can meet afterward."

"I wish for nothing more." She sounded relieved as she sighed. "Be careful, Robin. Rydon is a fair King. From what I gather, he intends to give you the location of the land where the battle will take place the night before."

"Why would he do such a thing?"

"Because he likes a challenge. If you are somewhat familiar with the battlegrounds, you won't be at as much of a disadvantage and the battle will not be so easily won or lost. Rydon believes victories must be earned and hard-fought."

It sounded as if Rydon thought of war like a game. Was slaughter entertainment for him? "He sounds like an interesting man, your King."

"You might like him if you were not on opposite sides."

"You are the only person in Iros I care to know." Hearing a clatter, he looked over his shoulder. It may have been a gust of wind, but he couldn't risk it. "I should go, Ari. I'll see you soon."

"Until then."

THE BATTLE WAS ON ITS THIRD DAY AND THE SOLDIERS hadn't much time to rest. Both armies would settle for a few hours to regroup, but they slept with one eye open.

Robin didn't know how much longer this would last. He hoped it would end soon because every time they stopped to take a breath, he thought of Arabella. He couldn't afford the distraction.

He sliced his way through several enemy soldiers before reaching one of their captains. It wasn't proper etiquette to involve oneself in another man's fight, but he couldn't leave one of his own to die. Each man bearing Queen Roanna's crest was now his responsibility.

He stepped in and took over the fight, blocking a blow to his head with his sword, and knocked the captain backward.

Robin's vision was spinning from an injury he'd sustained three nights prior; there was a gash on his head that hadn't been properly cleaned or dressed. It was hindering his ability to concentrate on the task at hand.

He blocked several more blows, one aimed at his knee and the other at his chest. He tried to strike at the captain's neck but his attack was blocked as well.

It couldn't have lasted for more than a few minutes, though it seemed like hours. They both managed to give the other a few scratches, but nothing that would win the fight.

Robin ducked as the captain's sword tried again for his head, and when he rose, there was another enemy soldier at his side. He swiftly delivered a fatal wound to the man's stomach, and in the time it took for Robin to turn back to his other opponent, the sword was nearing his throat and his reflexes weren't fast enough to block it.

Trystan struck the captain and left a gaping wound on the man's arm. Robin was able to move out of the way and the captain's sword hit a body at their feet.

Not wanting to interrupt Trystan's duel, he stayed out of the way and tried to go after lesser opponents.

He dodged some attacks and cut down others, but when he was finished, he returned to where the captain now lay dead at Trystan's feet.

"Thank you, old friend," Robin said breathlessly.

"Don't mention it. You look like hell." Trystan gripped his sword tightly as they surveyed the area.

There were more dead bodies than live ones, which meant

there were only a few men fighting still. The battle was dying down, though it was hard to say who had won.

"Do you think it's over?" Robin asked.

Trystan laughed, nudging the other with a shake of his head. "Go to her. I can handle this."

"Thank you. I'm appointing you as the acting Captain."

It wasn't entirely proper for him to leave without seeing an end to the battle, but he wasn't much good to them now. He had almost been killed and was no longer of use to his men. If it hadn't been for Trystan, he would be dead. It was better to stay out of their way.

He made the long walk back to camp and scribbled out his report. After seeing a physician to patch the wound on his head, he quickly washed up and changed his clothes.

He could hear other men returning to the camp, and the more voices he heard, the happier he was. From the sounds of laughing and cheering soldiers, it seemed as though they had officially won.

He didn't know what that meant, or what was next; all he knew was that he needed to see *her*.

After feeding and hydrating his falcon, he tied a note around its foot.

DEAREST ARABELLA,

THE BATTLE IS OVER! I MUST SEE YOU TONIGHT. WHERE SHALL we meet?

HE SENT THE FALCON ON ITS WAY AND ANXIOUSLY WAITED for its return. He was worried the falcon might not come back at all, or if it did, there would be no reply from Ari.

No one would know to contact him if something were to happen to her, unless by some miracle she had mentioned him to her friends.

He couldn't imagine never meeting her. It wasn't an option. After everything they had been through, alone and together, their rendezvous was well deserved.

He felt as though he had already seen her; like they had known each other lifetimes before and were merely becoming reacquainted.

As the sound of more men returning from the battle began to fill the camp, the falcon landed on its perch, and he held his breath.

ROBIN,

I AM BEYOND RELIEVED TO HEAR FROM YOU. I WAS SO WORRIED that I couldn't sleep. Meet me at the border. I'll be waiting.

SHE WAS SAFE. NOT ONLY THAT, BUT SHE WAS ALREADY ON her way to see him now. He scurried around to gather a few supplies in his bag and then he was off to ready Shadow.

He found Trystan in the stable tending to his own horse.

"I'm going to see her," he said breathlessly.

Trystan nodded as if he already knew Robin's destination. "Did you leave an address so that we can find you? You know, in case this is a trap."

Robin had never considered that. He may have been the temporary Captain of this army, but he didn't see why anyone would go through so much effort to kill him.

"Thank you for that vote of confidence," he said with a chuckle. "I'll be sure to give her your regards."

"Don't give her anything on my account. Be careful. We don't need to lose any more friends."

With a racing heart, Robin headed for the border. Near the edge of the kingdom, there was a stretch of land that was considered neutral; an extension of the Half-Points.

Most kingdoms had such borders on one side of their land. In the days of old, the border had been intended to house those seeking asylum, a waiting area until they had the approval of the reigning royal to enter the kingdom.

Anyone who wished to travel had to reach the border and then be ferried to the official lands of the Half-Points.

First used for asylum, and then for travel, it was now to be used as a home for a forbidden love.

His gaze scanned the area for any sign of her, but the darkness concealed most of his surroundings. Giving Shadow's mane a gentle pat, he took a deep breath and looked again.

There was a woman in the distance seated against a tree with her head in her hands.

He furrowed his brow and approached her cautiously. "Arabella?"

Lifting her chin, the woman wiped her cheeks and hastily got to her feet. "Robin?"

Most of her dark brown hair was tied up in a bun, though some strands hung loosely in her face. There was a jagged scar on the side of her neck. She had kind, hazel eyes, and though her cheeks were wet with tears, he had never seen anything more beautiful in his life. Her features matched her soul and everything he knew about her.

The other soldiers may have judged her for not wearing a dress, but he was perfectly content to see her in trousers and a tattered shirt. She was a warrior. Their kingdoms being at odds didn't change the pride in his heart upon seeing her.

Robin nodded to answer her question, and then took her hand in his. "Why are you crying?"

She was quiet for a moment as she gazed into his eyes. Then she threw her arms around him. "It doesn't matter now."

Robin smiled softly as he held her in his arms. Now he knew why so many songs and stories were written about this feeling.

Love.

He had never felt more at peace than when he was in her arms.

She pulled away and examined the gash on his head. "You're hurt. Why didn't you say something?"

"It's nothing. I wouldn't let a scratch keep us apart."

Arabella pulled something out of her pocket. She opened a container and revealed a salve, which she gently placed on his wound. "I'm not worth your life." After putting the salve back into her pocket, she stroked his curly hair. "You should have gone to see a surgeon."

"I was desperate to see *you*." He smiled sheepishly. "And I'm glad I didn't delay our meeting. I never thought anyone could be so beautiful."

In the light of the moon, he could see the blush on her cheeks as she looked away.

"Forgive me; are you not accustomed to compliments?"

"Do your brothers in arms usually comment on your looks?"

"No," he admitted with a laugh. "I understand your meaning. Should I avoid compliments in the future? Do they make you uncomfortable?"

"Not when they come from you." Arabella tilted her head, gaze wandering over his face as if to study it.

"What is it?"

"You are also beautiful. Has anyone ever told you that?" She closed what little distance there had been between them.

Their faces were mere inches apart. He couldn't stop looking into her eyes until his gaze was drawn to her lips. With confidence that the action would be warranted, he kissed her. He had never kissed anyone before and worried that his inexperience would be clear as day, but she wrapped her arms around him to deepen their mutual affection.

It was frightening and beautiful to explore each other's mouths with their tongues, though she seemed to have no trouble guiding him. They only pulled away to breathe.

"I don't understand how you fell in love without ever seeing me."

A smile graced his features. "I didn't need to see your face in order to love you. I fell in love with your soul. If others told me you were ugly, I would still find you beautiful." There was that word again, but she didn't seem to mind. "Besides, you hadn't seen my face either. I could have been a troll."

Arabella laughed and brushed her lips against his. "You are not like most men. And that is why I love you."

"I am like all the men I know. I live only to serve. I follow orders. The things I've seen, the things I've done..." He shook his head. "There's blood on my hands."

"Mine too. I've done things I'm not proud of. But that is the life of a soldier." Arabella's expression changed suddenly as she stared off into the distance. "I've stayed far too long. Meet me here tomorrow?"

She gave him a quick kiss and was then on her way before he had the chance to give her a proper goodbye.

He couldn't help but think that it was something he said. Had he scared her off? Was he less than what she'd been expecting? Being that he was a disappointment to himself, he could understand why Arabella would be disappointed in him too. Robin rode back to camp with dampened spirits, confused because when he'd left, they had been so high.

He walked to Trystan's tent and scratched the top of his head as he tried to make sense of what had happened.

"What is it?" Trystan asked. "Was she not as you'd hoped?"

"She was all that and more."

"Then why the long face?"

"I don't know." He furrowed his brow. "I suppose because...she left. And I wasn't ready to part from her."

Trystan rolled his eyes. "You are hopeless."

"Why do you say that?"

"Because you're in love. Although, I must admit, I knew that, out of anyone in our company, it would be you."

"Why, because I was hopeless to begin with?" he said with a laugh.

"No, because you are different."

"Oh." Robin pursed his lips. "She said that too. I don't know whether to take it as a compliment or an insult."

"It's a good thing, old friend." He smiled and patted his shoulder. "Trust me."

When night was upon them, Robin rode Shadow to where he had met Arabella the previous evening.

He dismounted his horse and tied him to the same tree Arabella stood against. As he kissed her cheek, warmth spread through his face. He was still unsure as to what was appropriate. They were more than friends, but they weren't technically lovers. What was considered the proper greeting for their situation?

"How are you tonight?" he asked.

"Just tired," she said with a smile. "Are you alright?"

Robin sat on the cool grass and she sat down beside him. "I wanted to talk about last night. I was worried I upset you."

"No, it had nothing to do with you. There was something I needed to take care of." Her hand rested over his.

"So, what I do, it doesn't bother you?"

She shook her head. "How could I judge your way of life? It's not something you chose. Besides, there's blood on my hands too. You're a good man, Robin...whether you believe it or not."

He nodded as if that settled the matter. There may always be a part of him that questioned his worth. Arabella was so far beyond anything he deserved. If she wanted him, he wouldn't argue, but there would be days when he questioned it.

"Tell me what you're thinking, Robin."

There was a twinkle in her eye that made his cheeks flush with color once more. His thoughts were innocent, but something about that look made him nervous. "I'd like to see where you're from."

"I'll show you Iros someday when King Rydon is in a better mood. He's touchy, that one. Quite rude and sometimes abusive to his subjects."

"Is that so?" He hardly knew anything about King Rydon. He had fought battles in Iros before, but he'd been nowhere near the royal castle. "Well, you'd better tell him that if he touches you, he will have to answer to me."

Arabella laughed. The thought must have been funny, him going against a king. "I'll be sure to tell him that." Their hands entwined as she rested her head on his shoulder. "Tell me more about yourself. I want to know everything."

"You know me in every way that matters." He shrugged. "There's not much to tell. I was taken from my home to serve my country. I was nine years old. The king was alive then and the policies are different now. Soldiers are not made quite so young. You could say that I'm a rare breed."

"I believe that. And is Daloran worth saving?"

"I hope so. I think I'm so busy defending it, I never have the time to actually see it or get to know the land and its people." He paused, gaze fixed on their hands. "Is Iros worth saving?"

"Truth be told, it has done nothing for me. But there are still good people there, so I fight for them."

He kissed the top of her head. "You have a good heart, Ari."

They sat in silence for a while, enjoying the feeling of being in each other's arms. Then Shadow became impatient, reminding them that the hour was late.

Arabella played with Robin's curls and then kissed him tenderly. "I will see you soon. Write to me until then."

He bid her farewell and watched as she went further and further away from him. He hated to watch her leave. They hadn't spent nearly enough time together. There was still so much to learn about each other, so much for them to discuss.

He hadn't even told her that he wanted to retire. What would she think of him being a domesticated Knight? Although, he wouldn't be a Knight at all if he was domesticated. That would defeat the purpose. His title would be stripped away.

Would she think less of him for wanting a simpler life?

Robin wasn't easily startled, but when he turned to see someone mere feet from him, he took a step back.

The man was dressed in a dark cloak, and if he hadn't known any better, he would have thought he was dreaming. The stranger had such a presence — one that Robin found overwhelming. The figure was powerful. He could sense that.

"Who are you?"

Robin was instantly uneasy. He was taught to sense others

so that no one could surprise him at camp or on the battle-field. Daloran soldiers were trained vigorously in order to avoid being ambushed.

The fact that this man stood there as if he had been watching them all this time left him unsettled, more so because Robin hadn't been aware of his presence at all.

"My name is Caym." The man's tone indicated that Robin had somehow inconvenienced him.

"What is it that you want?"

Caym approached him and removed his hood, revealing rugged features and an unpleasant scowl. He had copper eyes and ashen blond hair. "Stay away from Arabella. She's mine."

Robin furrowed his brow. "Arabella is a person, not a possession. She doesn't belong to anyone."

The man clenched his jaw. "All the same, she is not for you. I am involved with her."

"In what way?"

"I've known her far longer than you have. And I will not allow some lowly Knight to take her from me."

"Arabella is free to be with whomever she chooses. If I am her choice, you should respect that."

"If you love her, then love her enough to let her go. Her place is with me."

The furrow of his brow only increased as his disbelief mounted. "As I said, Arabella is free to make her own choice. What makes you so sure that she wants to be with *you*?"

"We have history," Caym hissed. "I loved her long before she ever knew you."

"And have you told her this?"

"She knows."

"If you confessed your feelings, and she is still with me, then she has made her choice."

"Do you think you deserve her?" Caym spat. "I can offer her the world! Can you do that, Robin of Daloran?"

"No, I can't. But Ari doesn't want the world. If you think she cares about material things, then you don't know her as well as you thought."

Caym's face turned red. For a moment, it looked as though steam was coming from his ears. "I'm giving you fair warning. Stay away from her."

Pulling the hood on his head, Caym disappeared into the night air. The ability to appear and disappear at will belonged to a select few known as sorcerers.

He couldn't understand why Arabella never mentioned this man. Whether they truly were friends, or Caym was delusional, he thought Arabella should have said something. The sorcerer was unstable, his anger seething and almost unnatural.

Whether it was him that Arabella wanted to be with or Caym, Robin was concerned for her well-being. It didn't seem as though she would be safe with the sorcerer even if there was love between them.

CHAPTER 4

"So, how did it go?"

Robin turned to face Trystan. The truth of the matter was on the tip of his tongue, yet he still didn't have the courage to divulge it to his friend. "It was wonderful. But then...something happened."

"Out with it."

"A sorcerer appeared to me after she left. Apparently, they know each other, and he claims to be in love with her."

"Ah." Trystan raised his brow. "So, Curly-Locks has some competition."

He shot his friend a glare. "This is no time for humor. Sorcerers have abilities beyond our wildest dreams."

"Do you think he's dangerous?"

"I don't know. I've only heard of those with magic, I've never dealt with them myself. I'm used to swords and fists, not mystical powers." Swallowing hard, he shook his head. "I fear for her. Something about him was unnerving. He threatened me."

Trystan furrowed his brow. "You should worry more for yourself and less for your lady friend. You don't know what he's capable of. Those with magic are unpredictable; no two are alike."

"The next time we see each other, I'll ask what she knows of him. If they're friends or...or something more—" He pursed his lips, gazed fixed on Shadow's mane. The horse was stomping the ground impatiently. "She may know about his abilities."

"And what if it so happens that the woman you love is in love with someone else?"

Robin mounted his horse and gave a light tug of the reins. "Then I wouldn't dream of coming between them."

"Robin," Trystan grumbled. "Do you realize you've never told me the name of this woman?"

"That's preposterous." No, it wasn't. "Of course I have." No, he hadn't. And it was becoming increasingly difficult to remain secretive.

"What aren't you telling me?"

"If I told you everything, you would wish I hadn't. Trust me."

He had plenty of time to ponder the situation as he rode toward the border. This time, his intent was to travel.

The ferry took him and Shadow to the Half-Point where the princesses awaited his company. They were housed on the largest property, protected by guards, and surrounded by tastes of Daloran; polished boulders, heaps of sand, and potted greenery.

With Shadow being taken care of in a nearby stable, he entered the extensive mansion and was led to a room where the royals were seated.

Food was laid out on the table and flames were crackling in the fireplace.

"Dearest Knight!" Bryony exclaimed as she embraced him. "It feels like forever since we last saw you."

Robin gave them both a hug before stepping away. "How are you? How is your mother?"

"Well..." Bry spoke quietly. "She wants peace, but King Rydon won't budge."

"Kings are fools to desire war. It is a terrible thing."

Prim took his hand gently. "We know you have suffered long for it, dear Robin."

"That is the duty of every soldier, to fight and, yes, sometimes suffer for their kingdom." The princesses encouraged him to be honest, but he still served the crown. He didn't want to speak out of turn.

"And we're sorry you have led such a life," Bryony said with volume in her speech again. "We hope it will not always be so. I'm sure our mother would release you from your duties if you were to ask. You have served us well!"

"I may do just that." While he had been meaning to speak with the queen for some time now, he couldn't bring himself to retire when she still had need of him. He didn't want Queen Roanna or the girls to feel like he was abandoning them. "I don't want to leave her so troubled."

"Mother's tired," Primrose said. "It can't be easy for her, running the kingdom alone, but we can't convince her to even entertain the idea of finding a new husband. We don't want a new king, you see, we simply want a companion for our mother."

"I understand. It must be lonely to rule alone. I think every person feels that way at some time in their lives."

"Yes, even princesses get lonely," Prim pointed out.

"You girls shouldn't have to worry about that. You're too young to marry."

"That's not true and you know it! You and Primrose are matched in age, and I'm not far behind." Bry giggled. "We haven't found any suitable partners yet. We hope that will change soon."

"When that time does come, I will gladly assess your suitors to be certain they are worthy of you."

"That's our Robin, always so protective!"

"So, Robin," Prim chimed in, "What about *your* love life? Did you ever meet that woman from your letters?"

"As a matter of fact, I have. And I'm happy to say that we are in love. I hope you will be able to meet her in the near future." A lump formed in his throat from lie after lie spilling from his lips. It wasn't all false; he did hope they would all meet under better circumstances someday, however delusional that hope may be.

Bry squealed with delight. "We are so happy for you! Tell us, what is it like to be in love?"

"It's the best feeling in the world. I've never been surer of myself, who I want to be, and what I want in life. I see things with such clarity, and empathy, even." He laughed and shook his head. "It's a difficult thing to describe."

"That's because love is a feeling, words won't do it justice. However, you've done very well." Bry beamed. "We can't wait to fall in love. We're hopeless romantics!"

Prim stepped away from the fireplace as her face appeared flushed. "There isn't much else for us to do besides reading and daydreaming. For now, that is."

"Stay young as long as you can." Robin couldn't remember the last time he'd felt youthful. Although he and Primrose were close in age, he felt as though he was her elder by many years. It was the nature of war. "I know someday you will rule over this land. That's why you have to live life to its fullest while you can. Enjoy yourselves without having the weight of the world on your shoulders."

"We will, Robin." Prim beamed at him. "And we hope *you* will learn to live without that weight."

He hoped so too. It had been his companion for so long, he wasn't quite sure he could give it up so easily. "I will. It will take some time, but it will happen. My love certainly has her work cut out for her."

Prim shrugged with an odd expression; there was something in her features he couldn't place. "I'm sure she has faults of her own. She can't be perfect."

"She is to me."

IT HAD ONLY BEEN A WEEK SINCE THEY'D LAST SEEN EACH other, but he hadn't told her about the sorcerer yet. Now was the chance, only, he wasn't sure how to do that without seeming offensive. It wasn't proper to ask a lady about her romantic relations, but he needed to know for his own peace of mind.

If it was Caym that she wanted, Robin needed to find a way to let her go.

"It seems like forever, doesn't it?" Ari approached with a smile and wrapped her arms around him.

All his doubts melted away when they were together. She brought him such peace. He couldn't imagine losing her, but if she was in love with another, it wouldn't be fair to make her feel as though she was beholden to him. "Too long, in my mind."

She pulled back only to kiss him. "How are you?"

"I missed you." He wanted to ask how *she* was before telling her about the sorcerer, but there didn't seem to be a way around it. "A friend of yours paid me a visit. His name was Caym, or so he said."

Arabella frowned. "Did he bother you?"

He was hesitant to tell her because he didn't want to cause a rift between them if they really were friends or something more. At the same time, if he was, in fact, dangerous, she had a right to be informed. "He threatened me, actually. He told me to stay away from you."

"He did *what*?" All color drained from her face as she shook her head. "I can't believe he did that. Did he say anything else?"

"That he's in love with you and has been for some time. He gave me the impression that I was getting in the way of your relationship." His gaze wandered over her for some sort of reaction; he couldn't read her. "Ari, if that's true...you know I only want your happiness. You won't ever have to see me again."

"Don't say that. I couldn't bear the thought." She took his hands in hers. "You're the one I love, Robin. Caym and I are old friends. I can't deny that I care for him, or that there was a time when I thought we could have been more, but that's over now."

He breathed a sigh of relief. "My only worry was that I was keeping you from your true love."

"You most certainly are not." She smiled softly, hands cupping his cheeks. "Caym is too late. I love you far too much to walk away."

Robin pressed his lips to hers as his arms secured around her waist. "Then I don't see why we should ever part again. I want to marry you, Ari. I want to live with you, to have children with you, to grow old with you. You would make me the happiest man alive by doing me the honor of becoming my wife, and I swear to you I will do everything I can to make you the happiest woman."

Ari stared at him for what seemed like hours. The color returned to her face and her fingers grazed his jawline. Finally, she grinned and nodded slowly. "Of course I'll be your wife."

Although he'd been hoping that would be her answer, he was still surprised to hear it. This all seemed like a dream, too good to be real. "Ari, I swear I'm going to spend the rest of my life trying to make you as happy as you've made me."

"There's no need." She pulled him closer to nuzzle his chest. "You've already done that."

He was so excited, his mind raced; he didn't know where to begin when thinking of their future. "We have to decide where we're going to live, I suppose. What are we going to do? And when are we going to do it?"

Arabella chuckled. "I suppose we'll decide when the time comes. We're not the first soldiers to marry." She paused and furrowed her brow. "Or are we?"

"I don't know, honestly." Pursing his lips, he glanced toward Shadow. "To tell you the truth, I've thought about retiring. I don't know how much fight I have left in me. Would you think less of me for that?"

"Heavens, no. I don't care what we do, where we make a living, or how we do it. As long as we're together, that's all that matters."

He breathed another sigh of relief. "I can't wait to tell my friends."

"I can't wait to tell mine!" She giggled. "Marriage is unusual for the Satari. I may not be the first to do it, but I know I'm one of very few."

Both smiles faded. Robin didn't have to ask what was on her mind; he already knew that their thoughts had settled on a similar place.

"Should we marry in secret?" he asked. "Run away together?"

"I don't want to hide. That would be a life of looking over our shoulders. I think we should come clean...and ask for mercy. I have faith that one of our rulers will be reasonable."

"And you're willing to give up your life in Iros if the more reasonable of the two is Roanna?"

"Yes. Are you willing to do the same if it's Rydon?"

"Yes. In some ways, I already have. My head and my heart reside with you. I suppose you can have the rest of me too." He smiled and rested his forehead against hers. "I am unapologetically yours."

"I don't want you to worry about a thing. No matter what the people in my life think of us, you are my priority now."

With her cheek against his chest, he was certain she could hear the erratic beating of his heart. It felt as though the vital organ was doing all sorts of new tricks; fluttering, skipping, and flying.

There was no better feeling in the world than hearing that he was important to the woman of his dreams.

His life, shrouded by war, death, and darkness, was coming to an end and beginning anew. For the first time, he could see light. It was the unfamiliar feeling of hope.

All the songs and tales of this feeling were wholly true.

Love could conquer all.

ROBIN KNEW THAT TRYSTAN WASN'T THE SENTIMENTAL type. He didn't care about grand gestures or important events, but Robin appreciated that his friend at least tried to appear happy for him.

"I'm not surprised," he spoke in a deep voice. "I always thought you were meant to be a family man. I can't say I'm happy to see you go, though."

"I would have retired even if I hadn't met her. I've been thinking about it for a long time. I just couldn't see a way out until she came along."

"Well, I think you're more progressive than the rest of us. Most of these men wouldn't know how to approach a woman, let alone marry one." Trystan paused. His face was scrunched as he seemed to struggle with saying the words. "Congratulations, old friend. I'm happy for you."

Robin nodded. He couldn't ask for more than that. "Thank you. And don't worry, we'll have a proper farewell with drinks and a feast before it's official."

"I assume that will happen after you return from the palace?"

"Yes. Once I have the queen's permission to retire, we will have a celebration." Gaze downcast, he fidgeted with his fingers. "Trystan, do you think less of me for leaving before the war is over?"

"Not at all, my friend. Get out alive while you still can." He patted the younger man's back with a smile. "I'm starving, so I'm going to the rather lackluster feast that awaits us in the mess tent. Will you be joining us?"

"I will, shortly. I want to finish packing."

Trystan vacated his tent and Robin returned to his belongings. He hadn't quite figured out how to break the news of Arabella's alignment. Truth be told, he had hoped the right words would come to him as he prepared for his departure.

He was concerned about getting word to Ari if the worst should happen and he was arrested. That wasn't out of the question; he'd accepted that risk, and so had she. But, like Arabella, he chose to have faith that someone would take pity on them.

He could hear roaring laughter from the mess tent, the cheering as a beloved song was being played, and even a disagreement or two — both were likely Trystan's doing.

Robin chuckled and shook his head. While he had come to appreciate those sounds, he wouldn't give up his new path for anything.

He turned to place a Telebird in his trunk and nearly walked into someone. They hadn't been there a moment ago.

He wondered if this was another sorcerer who could appear and disappear at will.

Swallowing with difficulty, he looked the man over, unable to recognize him. "Who are you and what are you doing here?"

"There is a matter we need to discuss."

This was no soldier. The stranger was dressed in robes and his hair was tidy.

His weapons were packed away in his trunk. He could attempt to retrieve one, but doubted that he could manage it in time. "What matter is that?"

"I urge you to stay away from Arabella Renatus. This is your final warning."

Robin furrowed his brow. "She loves me and I love her. I won't abandon her, not for anything."

"Even at the cost of your life?" The stranger raised his brow. "Is love really worth that price?"

"Without love, what is life? We are nothing without it. There is no hope, no light, and no future."

The man sighed with a shake of his head. "I don't want to do this. I'm giving you fair warning, and that's all I can do. Again, I urge you to leave her. You don't know what Caym is capable of."

Lifting his chin, he considered taking a step toward the trunk. Would the stranger notice? "I will not leave Arabella simply because Caym wishes it. His threats mean nothing to me. Ari means everything."

The man's gaze fell. "Are you certain you won't change your mind?"

"How many times must I say it? I love her, and she loves me. She's made her choice. We're going to spend the rest of our lives together. As long as she wants to be with me, nothing will keep me from her, not you, your master, nor anyone else. You tell him that."

The stranger paused and then gave a small nod. "You are an honorable man. I am sorry, but I have my orders. You've left me no choice."

Before Robin could question the meaning of that remark, the man pulled a sword from his belt and plunged it through Robin's chest.

He gasped for air as pain shot through him. The cold steel soon felt like fire in his lungs. Clutching the wound, he fell to his knees. He had been injured before, but nothing so mortal as this. It seemed as though the blade had stolen every breath left in his body.

By the time his gaze lifted to search for his attacker, the man was gone, and Irwing was standing in the opening of the tent.

The boy screamed for help and rushed to his side. Robin crumpled to the ground with the blade embedded in his lung.

"Sir, what happened? Who did this to you?"

"I don't know who he was," he croaked. "You must warn the others, Irwing. The enemy might be within our camp."

Tears streamed down the boy's cheeks. "They're calling for the medic, sir, I can hear them. It won't be long."

"No, Irwing." Robin could feel the blood soaking his shirt. He heard men clambering about and entering the tent, but his vision was fading. "I'm done for."

Blood gathered in his mouth. He tried to swallow it but there was far too much, and it spewed from his lips.

"What in the Queen's name—" With a bewildered expression, Trystan knelt beside him. "Help is coming, my friend. Just hold on."

"I can't..."

Blood was filling his lungs and he couldn't take a breath without the crimson liquid collecting on his tongue. The sound of his erratically thudding pulse was loud in his ears, nearly drowning out Irwing's horrified cries.

He would have given anything to stay, but death didn't work that way.

His vision blurring by the second, he struggled to picture every detail of Arabella's face. If he'd been given a choice, he would have wanted her to be the last thing he saw.

But death didn't work that way either. It was not convenient. It waited for no man. It cared not for needs, wants, or final wishes.

His body was panicking, fighting the battle to keep his heart beating, and losing. It only caused more blood to ooze from his wound.

Soldiers were taught to risk their lives and never fear death, but he was afraid.

This was the end and he hadn't been finished. There was so much left to do, to say, to see. He desperately wanted to live, but as hard as he was struggling to remain conscious, he had no say in the matter. This was out of his control.

Robin begged whatever higher power there may be to spare him, to give him another chance. He wasn't ready.

I don't want to die, he thought. *I don't want to die. I don't want to die!*

He could feel the separation of his soul leaving his body. It felt as though someone was ripping his very being from his earthly shell, forcing him to abandon every hope and dream that had ever been within his grasp.

Cold and darkness overtook his remaining sensations.

He had no choice.

Whatever air was comprised around him appeared pitch-black; a night sky without stars. Although nothing could be felt or seen, it seemed as though he was in a chair of some sort. Was that how the afterlife welcomed the dead, with a chair?

His head was in his hands as he tried to process the gravity of what happened.

He hadn't said goodbye to the woman he loved, the woman he was supposed to grow old with. He would never marry her, never have a family with her.

This was a cruel world indeed.

"Are you Robin?"

He furrowed his brow and raised his head to the unfamiliar voice. "Yes. Who are you?"

"I am King Rydon."

Robin studied him. The King's face didn't appear hostile, but this surely must be Hell. What sort of afterlife welcomed the dead by showing their enemies?

"Where are we?"

"Where people await judgement before they go to one place or the other."

"You mean Heaven and Hell."

"You catch on quickly."

Robin wondered about his own appearance, if his wound was evident, if his clothes were stained. King Rydon didn't appear dead at all, he looked quite fit and healthy. His hair was full and his eyes were bright. It occurred to Robin that he didn't know how the dead looked in the afterlife; perhaps it *was* normal to appear healthy and life-like.

"Did you die suddenly? Did the Daloran army defeat yours?"

King Rydon chuckled darkly. "No, I'm very much alive. Like the man who ordered your death, I am skilled in the art of magic." Noticing the look on Robin's face, Rydon quickly added, "I do not condone his actions, I assure you. I've come to make you an offer."

A king was going to make him an offer? Not just any king, his enemy, and a man who practiced strange magic that allowed him to appear to Robin in the afterlife. "What kind of offer?"

"Fight for me. If you agree to be a captain in my army, I can revive you."

Robin took a deep breath and then chuckled when he realized it was just out of habit.

He was quiet for a moment, though he didn't need time to think. He knew his answer. "I can't do that and you know it. My loyalty lies with Queen Roanna, with Daloran. I couldn't betray her even if I wanted to. She would have my head and your revival would be for naught."

"She might have done that just for loving my subject." King Rydon shook his head. "Once you enter our agreement, no one can kill you. I alone will have the ability to end your life."

None of his options sounded very appealing. He could stay dead or he could return to his life as, essentially, a prisoner. He didn't want to be controlled by someone. What kind of a life was that? "How do I know you won't kill me once I've served my purpose?"

His patience appeared to be wearing thin by the sigh that left his lips, but it wasn't obvious by the tone of voice. "It doesn't benefit me to kill you."

"And what of the assassin that murdered my Captain?"

"I trusted one of my associates with the task. The same one who murdered you. I told Caym to send a man who was meant to offer a chance for your Queen to surrender in order to spare her soldier's lives. Caym told the man to murder your Captain instead. It was a mistake."

"And yet, Caym walks freely enough to murder me as well. How am I supposed to trust you?"

"As I said, it was a mistake. However, Caym is far too valuable for me to punish him for one mishap. Your personal issues do not interest me."

"How did he know where our camp was located in the first place?"

"You are not the only soldier willing to betray your country for the promise of a new life. The answer lies within your camp. If it makes you feel better, we can sign a contract. I never break my word. Whatever you think of me, I am a man of honor. Just like you."

Robin sighed softly and placed a hand against his fore-head. He needed time to think about this, but he couldn't make a king wait. He didn't know how long this magic would allow them to converse. If he agreed to this, it would weigh heavily on his conscience. Loving Ari was one thing — fighting for the enemy was another. "It would be a great betrayal to the people I care about. It's better to stay dead."

Rydon's impatience showed in the breath he drew. His nostrils flared. "Very well. But know that if you choose to remain here, Arabella will not fare well."

Robin rose to face the king eye to eye. "Are you threat-ening her?"

"No, I would never harm one of my own," Rydon said hastily, "But without you, she will become so miserable that she will search for death at every turn, throwing herself into the most dangerous situations and going on suicide missions to end her suffering. You don't want that, do you?"

Robin's gaze fell to his feet. He imagined Arabella deliber-ately putting herself in danger. He imagined her putting up a believable fight, but letting her guard fall on purpose, and losing of her own free will. It was a thought he couldn't bear. "No...of course not. I would never want that for her."

"Then do we have a deal?"

Robin's gaze met the King's. He hoped that Primrose and Bryony would forgive him, and that Queen Roanna would understand.

Arabella's happiness was more important to him than his own life, but if the two were connected, he had no choice.

"Fine. I'll sign your contract."

CHAPTER 5

Robin opened his eyes and blinked to cure his blurred vision. He groaned and attempted to move his limbs, but they were heavy as boulders. The world around him was moving although he was not and it caused his stomach to lurch.

"It's alright," came a familiar voice. "Don't try to move. You're still on the mend."

He sat up slowly, and when his vision cleared, was greeted by Arabella's face. The Knight had never been happier to see her. She almost looked as miserable as he felt.

"You're here," he whispered.

"One of your friends found our letters and sent your falcon to me. I did not know the lengths Caym would go to, you must believe me..."

Robin furrowed his brow and outstretched his hand to brush against her cheek, but she pushed it away. "Of course I know that."

"Your brethren do not know where I've come from if that's what you're wondering."

He tilted his head and leaned in closer in the hopes that her gaze would meet his. It did not. "Ari, the only thing on my mind is you. You were my last thought when I died and my first thought when I woke. Your king revived me because of the love we have for one another."

"When I heard that your heart started beating again while they prepared for your burial, I had to see you. You deserve to know after everything you've been through."

Again, he reached for her hand but she pulled away. He couldn't fathom why she was being so cold. "Ari, what is it?"

"So much has happened since you've been gone. So much has changed."

If they had been preparing his funeral, he couldn't have been dead for more than three days. Otherwise, he would already be in the ground. How much could have happened in three days?

"Tell me."

"When I received news of your death, the first person I thought of was Caym. I went to him and…I realized that was where I wanted to be. It's where I belong. With him."

For a moment, he thought it was a nightmare, or that he was still dead, but she looked so real. This wasn't the place between Heaven and Hell, he knew what that looked like now. He was alive. He couldn't accept those words. "How long was I gone?"

"Not long," she spoke in a quiet voice. "I didn't mean for it to happen."

If he could have mustered the strength to move, he would have fled the tent. How could he have been so wrong about her? To judge her position would have been unfair. He couldn't know what he would have done in her place.

"I don't understand. You told me you felt nothing for him."

"I wasn't lying at the time." Still, she refused to meet his gaze. "He comforted me. He was there for me, and that's when I realized I do have genuine feelings for him. My guilt about what happened to you prevented me from acting on those feelings, but when I heard that you were given a second chance, I knew I was free to finally be with Caym."

His jaw clenched as he shifted on the bed; her nearness was far too much for his liking. His heart wanted to believe she had been genuine throughout their time together, but his mind convinced him otherwise. He was almost certain that, to some extent, Arabella must have been using him. She hadn't been successful in her mission. With his death, her assignment had ended.

That seemed like a far more logical explanation.

Rydon hadn't restored his life to save Arabella; he had manipulated Robin into switching sides. He'd fallen for their game.

"It was all a lie."

"No, please don't say that." Finally, her gaze met his, and it held tears. "I *did* have feelings for you."

"I understand perfectly. You told me that you never meant to fall in love, that you never wanted to. I should have known I was your mission and nothing more."

"You *became* more."

"But not enough." His nostrils flared as he shook his head. "You played me for a fool. Well done, Ari."

"No, Robin." Cupping his cheeks in the palms of her hands, her gaze searched his. "I loved you. It wasn't a lie. Our meeting was by chance."

It was as if she could read the suspicion in his mind. He had to wonder why she would bother to hold up appearances if she had never truly loved him. Perhaps he could believe that she hadn't been toying with him, but he was certain that King Rydon had taken advantage of their unique circumstances.

Swallowing the lump in his throat, he took in a shaky breath. "Then forgive me."

"For what?"

"Failing you."

Arabella's bottom lip trembled. "You didn't."

"I was careless. I was...weak." Turning his head caused her hands to fall from his face. "I died. And it changed everything."

"Believe me, it's better this way. We were chasing a dream and now we're awake."

"I prefer the dream."

She smiled tearfully and rose to her feet. "Goodbye, Robin. I'm so sorry for all of this."

He wanted to take her hand but thought better of it. "None of this is your fault. You deserve the greatest joy and I cannot give you that."

Arabella exited the tent and the pain throughout his body grew exponentially. If she was happier without him, he should let her go.

He *should*.

And yet, he was compelled to rise from his bed and follow her out of the tent, only someone pressed a hand to his chest as he reached the opening.

The man had black hair and dark eyes. He looked stern, and his demeanor made Robin feel cold. "I'm sure this is difficult for you, but you need to stay away from her. You have to respect her decision."

Robin nodded without a word as he watched the stranger walk away with the love of his life.

ROBIN SQUEEZED THROUGH THE CROWD OF PEOPLE WHO surrounded his tent to get inside. He felt overwhelmed by the attention. They gawked at him as if he was a means of entertainment. He was a living, breathing being with feelings, and they continued to look at him as if he was a ghost.

It would be impossible to overcome what had happened if the camp was constantly welcoming strangers to get a look at him. The resurrected man. The undead one.

No one knew what to call him. Robin himself didn't know what he was; human or something else?

He was relieved to see Trystan standing near his bed.

"What are they all doing here? You would think I was royalty or something."

"They're in awe of you. You came back from the dead. They want to know more about you and your experience. You're a miracle."

"I wish I wasn't," he grumbled. He heaved a sigh and scratched his head. "I can't be the first person who's ever come back from the dead."

"Probably not. But you're the first, and more than likely *only,* person they'll ever see in their lifetime."

Robin didn't know the history of magic or how many others had been brought back to life. He wondered how rare it was. Were there others like him? "Well, I can't do anything for them. I don't know what they want from me."

"They don't understand, that's all." Trystan cleared his throat and it took him a moment to make eye contact. "I suppose it's something everyone wants to know. What it's like to die, I mean."

Robin folded his arms. "Are *you* asking, or are *they*?"

"I am."

He'd been anticipating the question, but that didn't make it any easier to answer. Soldiers were lonelier than anyone else in the kingdom; their lives were filled with turbulence, sorrow, and death. Many would be overjoyed to be given a second chance. Robin longed to return to the grave.

Anything was better than this shame. Anything was better

than the misery he would face every single day knowing that he was betraying his country and, more importantly, his friends.

"It's cold...and lonely. It happens so quickly. It was dark where I was. I don't know if it was because of how I died, or because of my state of mind, but I felt no peace."

Trystan wore no expression, giving no indication of his thoughts. "So, there is no peace after death?"

"I'm not saying that." Without being able to read his friend's blank features, Robin struggled to understand what the man was looking for. Was he concerned for Robin's well-being, or was he searching for hope that the afterlife would be pleasant? "I do believe there is peace. There was none for me at that moment, and I didn't stay long enough to know what happened afterwards. I didn't want to die. I wasn't ready. I think that is why my experience was so dismal."

Trystan nodded. It was rare to know how his friend truly felt in any situation, but Robin was grateful that he was making an effort. "I'm sorry for what happened to you, Robin. I cannot imagine what you've been through, and I'm glad you're back. You're the only friend I have. So, please don't do that again."

Robin rubbed his jaw to prevent it from falling ajar. Trystan had never been so open with him. There had been times when he'd wondered if Trystan had even considered him a friend. Now he knew, and it was a relief that he wasn't wrong about their friendship. "Thank you. That means a lot to me. You've always looked out for me, Trystan. I will never forget the kindness you showed me when I was a trainee."

"That was for purely selfish reasons. I saw myself in you. No one helped me when *I* was a trainee, so..."

He smiled and shook his head. "Helping someone else without the expectation of reward is the opposite of selfishness. I may have been the first and last person you took under your wing, but it still counts as an act of kindness."

Trystan growled and scrunched his nose. "Then you were lucky to come to us at a time when I was vulnerable. I don't think I would extend the same helping hand if you were to come to us now."

"All the same, I am grateful for our friendship." Robin paused and pursed his lips. "No, more than that. I consider you a brother."

"Lucky for both of us that you came to the camp when you did." A hint of a smile crossed the older man's lips as he patted Robin's back. "Otherwise, I would not have a single friend."

"Lucky indeed. Your friendship has been the only good thing I've experienced during my time as a soldier."

"The *only* good thing? What about the woman who came here?" He raised his brow. "I believe her name is Arabella."

"It is." Robin swallowed with difficulty. His friend finally knew her name after months of secrecy, and he prayed that Trystan would never learn the truth about her. "Arabella left me for the sorcerer I told you about."

"The one who sent the assassin to murder you?"

"Indeed."

Trystan's brow furrowed. "She's with someone else, after everything? The day you died, she stayed with your body well into the following night. I witnessed her despair. That doesn't make sense."

"Well, that's what happened." He shrugged to make it seem insignificant, but he was dying inside. Too melancholic to cry. Too exhausted to sleep. The sadness ran too deep for him to be able to produce tears. His resurrection had a strange effect that made him wonder why he'd come back at all. This life after death was worse than the life he'd had before, certainly worse than death itself. "She said she loves us both, but she loves him more. And it took her all this time to realize it."

"That's quite strange. Not that I have much experience with women or the intricacies of their minds..." Shaking his head, he heaved a sigh. "I'm sorry to hear of it. I know how much you care about her."

"It's a difficult thing to wrap my mind around. At first, I thought she was lying, but...I've never known her to lie." He paused to rethink that statement. Did withholding her profession count as a lie? He had known her origins, but not her allegiance. "I don't think I ever really knew her, Trystan. And I will never forgive myself for being so blind."

"Oh, come now." Clicking his tongue, he gave Robin another pat on the back. "If love is what you seek, I have no doubt you will find it again when you're ready. When Queen Roanna learns that you died in the line of duty, she may even grant you an early retirement."

"Hmm." It was more likely that she would execute him than release him. "I think you overestimate her mercy."

"Don't be so glum. Whatever happens, I will remain at your side, as always. And I want you to know that you can come to me if you need to talk. I'm an expert listener, you know this."

Robin chuckled, pleasantly surprised by his friend's momentary jovial demeanor. It was a most welcome change to their typical dreary attitudes. "Thank you. You're a good friend."

HE WAS DRESSED IN HIS FINEST AND UNBEARABLY NERVOUS. It was rare that he was granted an audience with the queen. She had a busy schedule and only met with people when it was of the utmost importance. Normally, a secretary or some other appointed official would handle matters such as this, but because he was close to the hearts of the princesses, the queen wanted to speak with him personally.

Robin should have felt honored, but the guilt was eating away at him. He betrayed the queen and her daughters. He had betrayed all the men who fought and died in battle over the years. He was working for the enemy because of his own selfish need to be alive.

He gave a forced smile and bowed when Queen Roanna entered. She sat upon her throne; the seat making the tall woman appear smaller than she was, minimizing the grandness of her stature. Her emerald gaze was piercing and her demeanor was unnerving.

"Good day, Sir Robin. It seems we have important matters to discuss."

He could tell her everything at this very moment and face the consequences. The weight would be lifted and his fate, whatever it may be, would be sealed. Something told him not to. Perhaps it was his survival instinct, the one reminding that the queen could have him imprisoned. He couldn't say a word about King Rydon or the deal that was struck. "I wish to retire, Your Majesty."

She paused as her gaze wandered over him. His hands were fidgeting behind his back out of anxiousness. He wondered if she could sense that something was wrong.

After a moment, she smiled and nodded. "Of course you do. You have served this country well. Might I ask why you wish to end your promising career?"

"I want to live out my life as normally as I can. In peace. I want to experience things that I haven't had a chance to. I just...want to live."

"Of course you do," she said again in the same musing tone. "I expect someday you'll want a family. I understand that must be a difficult thing to do in the army."

"I fear, if I force myself to fight for much longer, my heart would not be in it, and I would make mistakes at the cost of others."

"You're one of our best, Robin. We will all be sad to see you go. But your request is granted."

The compliment brought a flush of red to his cheeks. No strings attached, no final mission to carry out. It was so easy that he worried it may have been a trap. None of this seemed to match what he knew of her reputation. Could it be that the queen had changed her ways? "Thank you, Your Majesty. It has been an honor to serve you."

Before she had a chance to retract the statement — or to see right through him and directly to the betrayal in motion — he turned to leave, but her voice stopped him.

"I heard you had a brush with death. What a thing that must have been to endure."

"More than a brush, I would say." He swallowed hard and then turned to face her. "It was difficult, Your Majesty. But it's over now."

"My daughters were worried about you. We're all relieved to see you safe."

"Thank you." They had never discussed personal matters. And what could be more personal than death? His interactions had been with the princesses only, adding to the ever-growing paranoia that those around him had knowledge of the conditions regarding his return. "It's not an experience I'm keen to repeat anytime soon."

"How is it that you were able to return to the land of the living? I presume it was by magic, since I have yet to learn of another way."

Sweat formed on his brow that he hoped was hidden by his curls. "I couldn't see their face. It was a man by the build, I think. They stated that one day they may ask me a favor, and then they disappeared. I didn't even have time to thank them."

"How very fortunate we are. The kindest acts come from strangers." Her head tilted, gaze never straying from his as one corner of her lips turned upward into a crooked smirk. "I do hope you see that person again. I would like to reward them."

"If I recognize them, I will tell them so." It made him feel sick to his stomach to lie, but what choice did he have?

Robin bowed before exiting the room and making his way to the royal gardens. He took in several shaky breaths to regain control of his erratic breathing; desperately needing the fresh air. He was suffocating, the world around him over-whelming his senses.

He thought he might faint when he heard two familiar voices.

"Robin!" they called after him.

He smiled as they ran into his arms. The princesses were sights for sore eyes. He hugged them both as best he could. "It's good to see you both."

"When we heard what happened, we couldn't believe it!" Bryony spoke with tears in her eyes. "We said, *'not our Robin, it can't be'*. We were just beside ourselves...but now you're back."

"It must have been terrible for you." Prim's voice broke.

He stepped back to gain a better view of them. "No more tears on my behalf. It was something I'll never forget, but it's over now. I'm alright."

"Mother wants to reward whoever saved your life." Bry wiped her eyes on the sleeve of her dress. "She knows how much you mean to us."

"I'm sorry to worry you. I'll try to stay out of trouble from now on."

"Arabella must be so relieved," Prim said. "If *we* were heartbroken, I can't even imagine how she must have felt."

The words brought instant tears to his eyes. The pain he'd been struggling to bury was brought to the surface, making it a task to even breathe, let alone speak. The ache in his chest was insurmountable.

"I don't think she felt much at all," he began, "Because we're not together anymore. She's with someone else."

"What?" Bry said breathlessly. "What happened? I thought things were going so well."

"I thought so too. But she came to the realization that she had feelings for another man, and there's nothing I can do about it."

"Yes, there is." Prim folded her arms with a scowl. "You can fight for her. I can't believe you'd give up so easily."

"Well, I..." Robin furrowed his brow. He hadn't even considered that. "I'm not sure that's the right thing to do. She wants nothing more to do with me. Shouldn't I respect that?"

"You could, or you could make her realize that she made a huge mistake choosing this other man. Who is he, anyway?"

It was information he hadn't intended to share, but with so many other secrets between them, he wanted to share some semblance of truth. "She's with the man who murdered me."

Their mouths fell agape, eyes wide and unblinking.

"I know," he stated with a sigh. "I don't understand it either."

"I will support you in whatever you decide," Prim spoke quietly. "Just know that I don't like this, not one bit. I don't know how she can be with that man after what he did to you."

"Maybe she never cared for me at all."

Bry gripped his slumping shoulders. "Don't give up, Robin. If you don't fight for her now, you might wish that you had later. Don't have any regrets."

"She's right," Prim agreed. "You wouldn't be our favorite Knight if you gave up without a fight."

He still wasn't sure it was a good idea. He could come out of this looking like a complete fool, and Arabella could hate him. It could tarnish everything he thought they'd shared. He didn't want that.

However, the princesses made a good point. There was nothing left to lose.

"Thank you both," he spoke quietly. "I must be off. I expect the army is waiting for news about the queen's decision."

"Oh, do be careful." Bry kissed his cheek. "I wish you didn't have to return to Iros at all."

"Well, if I am to fight for Arabella, I have no choice but to go back."

CHAPTER 6

If he hadn't known better, he would have thought Caym was a king. His home was like a fortress. It was three stories high and had many rooms, judging by the number of windows. It was made of the finest stone, not just any old rocks that could be found in a field. There was a fence around the perimeter, well-made from a mixture of boulders and wood. He wondered if there were enchantments to keep unwanted visitors out.

Sure enough, as he tried to take another step toward the gate, a jolt went through his body and he was thrown backward.

He grimaced and got back on his feet. It wasn't a pleasant feeling, but he had felt worse.

"Arabella!" he shouted. "I need to speak with you!"

There was no answer, not that he'd expected one.

"Arabella, please! We have to talk! Don't leave it this way!"

He shouted until his lungs were sore and his throat was dry, and then he shouted some more. It seemed to take hours before the gate opened and someone appeared. It was the man who had walked away with Arabella.

"You need to leave," he said in a stern voice.

"I don't believe we've been properly introduced. My name is Robin Durand."

"I'm Galen Kelt," the stranger responded. "And I'm Arabella's friend. She doesn't want to see you."

"I'm not leaving until I know she's happy."

"And what makes you think she's not?"

"I worry she's not being honest with me."

Galen narrowed his gaze. "Arabella doesn't lie. Whatever she told you is the truth. You just can't accept it."

"Our love wasn't one-sided; I know it wasn't. Do you expect me to believe her feelings changed in a matter of days?"

"It doesn't matter what you believe," Galen grumbled. "All that matters is that you take Arabella at her word. Leave her alone."

"She couldn't have faked that kind of emotion. I know she still loves me, and I'm not ready to give up on her."

"That's not your decision to make." Taking a step forward, his chin lifted, narrowed gaze unrelenting. "I know her better than anyone. Her feelings *have* changed." Galen flexed his hand, gave a pause, and then relaxed it. "She may have loved you, but love is fleeting. In my opinion, she likely fooled herself into thinking that she loved you when what she truly wanted was Caym."

Robin shook his head. "As I said, I'm not leaving until I see her. I need to know she's happy."

Speaking through gritted teeth, he gripped Robin's shoulder tightly. "You are an arrogant, selfish, desperate man. She doesn't want to see you. You're not helping her, you're *hurting* her. And if you hurt her, you'll have to answer to me."

Robin had no intention of fighting this man. He didn't know if Galen knew what he and Ari had shared, but he clearly didn't understand. "I'm not giving up on her. I'm going to fight for her."

Galen's grip tightened. "Do you have any idea how pathetic you sound? She doesn't want you. Get that through your thick skull. If you don't leave her alone, I'll kill you myself."

"Go ahead." Robin shoved Galen's arm away from his own. "I've died once for her already. I think I can do it again."

Galen shook his head, gaze full of the deepest disdain. He looked as though he wanted to say or do something more, but must have decided against it, and walked back to the gate.

Robin took a deep breath and surveyed his surroundings. He contemplated whether or not to stay outside Caym's home. If it was true that his presence would alarm Arabella, it was better to spare her the conflict.

There was only so much he could do; only so many times he could try before it became too much. All he wanted was closure for the both of them. He owed it to their relationship — even if that turned out to be merely a deep friendship — to be unequivocally certain she was all right.

It was one thing to make a confession during times of high emotion; it was another to maintain façades consistently.

THERE WAS A CHILL IN THE AIR. HIS GAZE SURVEYED THE area, watching various wildlife from afar. The sound of normal activity in the camp was behind him. Their voices were a stark reminder of the betrayal he was soon to commit.

It wasn't too late; he could refuse to carry out King Rydon's orders, but he was a man of his word. If rumors of the king's temper were true, he didn't want his stubbornness to result in the harm of those dearest to him.

His life didn't matter; he could go back on the agreement and return to the afterlife. But what of Arabella's happiness? What of Trystan's, or that of every other man in their camp?

He could choose to be noble. Or he could do the most difficult thing he'd ever done and attempt to save lives by doing so. Robin would have the king's ear and hoped to sway him in one way or another. This could benefit Daloran if he was clever about it; a soldier working both sides without either knowing that he was doing so.

No matter what the outcome, he knew that it would not end well for him. He was playing a game only to lose.

There would be no pardon, no peace, and no love. Even his honor and dignity would be stripped from him. It was a lonely path he was to embark on.

"Where will you go?"

Inhaling sharply, he turned to see Trystan standing beside him at the top of the hill. "I'm not sure. I've considered living on one of the Half-Points."

"You always did love those places."

"I may not be able to own endless acres of land, but I don't need it. All I want is a home." Smiling softly, he turned back to gaze at the grazing wildlife below. "Will you miss me?"

"Some." Trystan cleared his throat. "It's very brave, what you're doing."

"Surviving?"

"Leaving the army. It's rare for soldiers to live beyond serving and do something with their lives."

"I remember when they said it would never happen for me. That I was too young."

"And look at you now." He clapped Robin on the back. "You've been granted early retirement."

"Yes. All I had to do was die for my country." The weight of his words hadn't been considered before he'd allowed them to leave his lips. It left an ache in his chest. "It's not lost on me that no other soldier has been afforded the same opportunity."

"Do you think the queen has other plans for you?"

"I don't know. It's possible she's being kind by allowing this. And I have favor with her daughters. But I can't help wondering...why *me*?"

"Perhaps you're not as good a soldier as you thought, so there was no reason to keep you." Trystan nudged his arm.

"Ah, yes." He chuckled and shook his head. The other was not one for humor; it came few and far between. Robin was grateful whenever Trystan's playfulness appeared. "That must be it."

"Don't question it, my friend. Enjoy it."

Heaving a sigh, he shifted his weight onto one hip. "Will you be alright?"

"That remains to be seen." Trystan looked over his shoulder. "The men are uneasy. There's a traitor in our midst. Someone gave away the position of our camp. That assassin knew where to find you."

"Yes. I imagine the army will retreat after that incident."

"For now. But that is not your concern." His voice lowered. "I wish you would stay, Robin."

Furrowing his brow, he turned to face his friend. "Why?"

"What if the assassin returns?"

"Trystan, I was murdered in my own camp, surrounded by the queen's army. Staying will not protect me. In fact, if I am the target, it will only put the rest of the men in danger."

"And if something happens to you during retirement, how will I know?"

"You're my brother, Trystan. In the event of my death, you are the only person I would have notified. There will be a falcon for you."

"So, you truly have given up on Arabella."

Robin paused to consider his answer. "I think... I'm still confused. I don't quite understand what happened; if she truly loved me and simply loved Caym more, or if she was manipulating me the entire time."

"Best to keep your distance then," he spoke in a gravely tone.

"Why do you say that?"

"Don't tell me you haven't thought of the possibility that she may have given away our position and sent the assassin." Turning back to face the wilderness, he folded his arms. "I know she lives in Iros, Robin. I'm not a fool."

His mouth suddenly felt dry. The trembling of his hand was only masked by the clenching of his fist. "We never discussed our locations, only where we were born. Iros knew we would invade eventually. They could have had scouts waiting in every corner of the kingdom to determine where we were. It doesn't mean Arabella was responsible."

"It doesn't mean she *wasn't*."

"I agree."

"The only reason I haven't reported your correspondence is because I don't believe it had any bearing on the outcome of the battle. If I thought your relationship had been a means to an end..."

"You would have turned me in like a good soldier." He loosened his fist. "I know."

Trystan lowered his chin, arms falling to his sides. It was the first time Robin had ever seen him appear truly disheartened. "Does being a good soldier make me a terrible friend?"

"Not at all," he assured. "I don't know what I would have done in your position."

"Anyway..." Chin lifted, he scratched the back of his head. "We may never know her true intentions. If she was a spy or if there's a traitor in our army. Either way, it's better to be rid of her. The fact remains that you were murdered because you fell in love with her."

Robin nodded slowly. "You hold her responsible for my death."

"Yes."

"The fault lies with the man who killed me. Not Arabella."

"If you won't stay away from her for your own sake, then do it for mine." Trystan turned to his side and Robin did the same. "I can't lose you again. Promise me you won't try to win her back."

"I'm not trying to win her back. Not exactly." He met Trystan's gaze briefly before it fell. "I haven't seen her since she left me. It feels...unsettled."

"I'm here to be the voice of reason. Relationships end, sometimes badly, and there isn't always a reason. To the heartbroken, there is no answer that will seem satisfactory. This is something you may never know." His brow raised. "Do you think you can live with that?"

"Yes," he said quietly. "If she won't speak to me then...I'll have to take her at her word." Aware he should have done that very thing in the first place, his head hung low. It was a fragile time in his life. His world had been shattered in more ways than one. He couldn't be certain that his mind and instincts were as sharp as ever. His actions may not be practical, but love was not a sensible thing. "I'll try to speak to her in a few days. I suppose I'll see what happens then."

"Good." Trystan patted his back. "Then you won't mind showing up to your going-away party."

"My *what*?"

"We're having a little gathering. It's not every day that a fellow soldier dies...and then lives to retire peacefully." He gave a definitive nod before walking off. "It's at eight o'clock tomorrow evening. Don't be late!"

ROBIN STARED AT THE WELL-LIT TENT AND BRIEFLY
contemplated returning to his own. Being social was the last
thing on his mind. His miraculous return from the dead had
made him all the more distrusting of people. The secrets in
his life were difficult enough to hide as it was, and they
seemed to keep building.

How long until it became too high? How long until it all
came tumbling down?

Disappointing his friends was out of the question, so he
put a smile on his face and walked inside.

Derynk immediately handed him a drink while Simian
handed him a plate of food.

"I hope you're hungry!" Simian said. "We have enough
here to feed an army."

The laughter of everyone inside the tent was immediate,
and Robin couldn't help but laugh with them. "Thank you all
for coming. A man with so many friends is a rich person
indeed, although, *actual* coin wouldn't hurt at the moment."

Irwing cleared his throat, his voice strained as he tried to
speak over everyone else. "What will you do for employment,
sir?"

"I'm deciding between being a physician and a tailor.
Those are the only other skills I possess."

"Perhaps you'll see us again after all!" Derynk spoke with a
laugh. "The army is always in need of stitching up...in both
fashions!"

Every man in the tent agreed with a roar of laughter.
There wasn't a single person who didn't have rosy cheeks or
glazed-over eyes. They had all been drunk before his arrival
and he considered himself fortunate for that; it meant he
would be able to slip away without anyone noticing.

Trystan tugged him toward a table in the corner and

patted his shoulder before they sat down. "You did well," he said in a hushed tone. "They have no idea how upset you are."

"Is it that obvious?" Robin whispered back.

"Only to me. Don't worry." Trystan's gaze wandered over him. "It's overwhelming for you, isn't it?"

"I don't know how to explain it." Head lowered, he crossed his arms over his chest. "I feel more alone than I ever have before, you see. And no one has done anything to make me feel that way. Everyone has gone out of their way to cele-brate my return, in fact. I didn't know how many of them cared I existed until...I came back."

"That's why you feel alone, my friend. No one will ever understand what you've been through. You've had an experi-ence that is unique in the best of ways, and the worst." He gave Robin's shoulder a squeeze. "You've always seen the world differently. And more so now."

He cleared his throat so that it wouldn't break when he spoke. "Thank you all the same. It was thoughtful of everyone to give me a proper send-off."

"You will be missed, but not by me. I'm going to be around to check on you from time to time."

"I'll hold you to that." Tears brimming his eyes, he averted his gaze, thinking that, if he avoided facing his friend, the emotion would go unnoticed. "You've been my greatest friend through all these years, you know. No, you've always been more than that. You're my brother, Trystan. Even with the years between us, we've understood each other in ways no one else ever could."

The older man moved closer, bumping his shoulder with Robin's. "I'm sorry you're alone in this. No one will know the burden you carry, but I see it. And I will always lend you my ear. A shoulder to cry on, should you need it."

The discovery of his betrayal was inevitable. Sooner or

later, someone would learn the truth. In his mind, he had already lost everyone and everything he cared about.

Time simply hadn't caught up with him yet.

For all he knew, this could be the last conversation they ever had on civil ground.

Swallowing hard, he wiped the corner of his eye. "Thank you, brother. I will miss you."

"Don't say it like that." Trystan chuckled and nudged his arm. "It sounds like you're saying goodbye."

✿❦✿

ROBIN POUNDED A NAIL INTO THE FLOORBOARD AND cursed when it damaged the wood. With this being the most emotional time in his life, it wasn't the best idea to do construction, but he didn't have a choice.

No longer in the queen's employ, he needed shelter; a roof over his head. It was time for him to learn how to be self-sufficient.

He'd never built anything in his life, but he purchased books to guide the design of what he hoped would be his forever home.

Robin heard Trystan's chuckle as he was given a hammer with a more suitable head for the task. "Need a hand?"

"Or ten," he answered with a laugh. "I think I've taken on more than I can handle. I thought I could do it on my own, but perhaps I should have *bought* one instead."

"Nonsense." Trystan handed him another tool. "If you can win wars in the queen's name, you can certainly build a house."

"I'm not so sure about that. There will be holes in the roof and the house will cave in on me in no time. Just you wait!"

"And if that happens, you'll rebuild. Or buy a house and

save yourself the trouble." He paused. "You're not doing this for Arabella, are you?"

Stepping back to criticize his handiwork, Robin shook his head. "No, I'm doing this for me. I need a place to live. A home of my own. I had dreamed of building a life with her, but that's not up to me."

"When are you going to attempt to speak with her next?"

"In two days' time. I'll leave tonight."

"I should go with you," Trystan grumbled.

"There's no need, truly."

"Robin, don't be a fool. So far, you're safe here at the Half-Point. Soon, Queen Roanna's army will withdraw, and we will not be in a position to help you in any way. Arabella could take you prisoner or deliver your head to the King of Iros for the notoriety. You may not care whether or not you die again, but I do."

"I'll be careful, Trystan. If anything untoward happens, I'm sure you will be informed."

Gesturing for his friend to follow, Robin walked the property line. He had five acres of land all to himself. For most, that would have been an unsatisfactory amount, but he didn't need much. The land was blessed with lush grass, thick trees, and unkempt gardens of flowers that had spread throughout most of the property.

It needed a house and some tidying up, but it was home. There was peace simply in that knowledge.

"You could have more land elsewhere," Trystan mumbled. "Anywhere, in fact."

"I'm not a farmer. I'll have a garden, to be sure, and that's all. This is quite generous for a Half-Point."

"Others have more land here, don't they?"

"They do. I am not a greedy man. I don't need much."

"I know that. But you deserve it. What if you outgrow this place?"

"I very much doubt that. If I do, I suppose I'll have to sell it and move." Stepping over a patch of thyme, he laughed as Trystan trampled through it.

"Sorry," he said with flushed cheeks. "You've always had more grace."

"That's not true. I simply pick up my feet when I walk."

"No, you pay attention to the simplest things. You notice what most take for granted."

Robin's brow furrowed. Since his return, Trystan had been praising him. While the other had always bettered his self-esteem, it had never been so consistent. "Is there a reason you're being so complementary?"

"When people say you don't realize what you have until it's gone, it's true." He stopped walking, hands connected behind his back. "You died and I realized you were my only friend. And I took you for granted. That will never happen again."

With a small smile gracing his usually solemn features, Robin placed a hand on his friend's shoulder. "Thank you, Trystan. I hope that you understand what your friendship means to me."

And how devasting it will be when I lose it, he thought.

The older man gave a firm nod before they continued walking the line of the property. "You should know that the men haven't given up on finding the spy."

He nearly stopped in his tracks. The fist concealed from Trystan on the opposite hip clenched. "What spy?"

"Don't play coy with me. A spy is the only reasonable explanation for your assassination and you know it."

"I don't want the men looking for trouble on my account."

Both ceased their steps as Trystan turned to him, nostrils flared. "Do you truly have such disregard for your own life?"

"I know what it means to die. I know what comes after this life. The worst has already happened to me."

"And if there is a spy in our midst, others will suffer the same fate." His chin lifted, eyes narrowed while staring Robin down. "Only they will not be as lucky as you were."

He shook his head, gaze unfaltering. "I wouldn't call it luck."

"Neither would I. It was a miracle." With a wave of his hand, he stepped back to create distance between them. "The others may believe some mystical stranger helped you on the assumption that they *may* one day ask for a favor, but I'm no fool. This was no random act, was it?"

Releasing a weary sigh, Robin pinched the bridge of his nose. "What would you have me do?"

"Tell me the truth!"

"A stranger *did* save my life."

"At what cost? Has the favor already been asked? Has the price already been paid?" As Robin attempted to walk away, Trystan grabbed his arm. "You forget that I know you, brother. I can *see* the weight you carry. The burden was heavy before, but it's crushing you now. It's killing you inside, isn't it?"

"Leave me." All the courage in the world wouldn't help him to meet his friend's gaze. He was afraid that if the conversation continued, he might, indeed, tell the full truth. "*Please*."

"Did you have to give up your love to save your life?"

"I had to give up *everything*." Tearing his arm from Trystan's grasp, he walked in the direction of the unfinished house. "I wish I hadn't come back."

Trystan followed. "How can one who has experienced death wish to return to it?"

Robin gave no answer.

They remained in silence until the older man had mounted his horse, ready to depart.

Robin still could not meet his gaze. Instead, he focused on Shadow's mane, shaking fingers combing through it.

"I hope you think better of your life, my friend. It is a gift. You've been granted your freedom. Do not waste it."

Listening to the sound of Trystan's horse retreating from his land, he waited until they were out of sight before sniffling.

Eyes filled to the brim, his vision blurred while hand patted Shadow's neck. "I fear that even you will abandon me in the end. And you would be right to."

CHAPTER 7

He waited for hours. It took all day of him pacing, walking the perimeter, and shouting every so often to get someone to come out of the manor.

Robin held his breath as he saw Arabella walking toward him. The sight of her brought tears to his eyes. Seeing her was the very reason he'd been so persistent, and yet, he was unprepared for the sight of the woman who had both blessed and cursed his existence.

He quickly blinked away the tears and hoped she wouldn't notice them. "I was hoping we could finish our conversation. You left so abruptly."

The air between them was filled with tension. Ari's fists were clenched and she took several deep breaths. "You're going to get yourself killed if you keep coming here."

"I don't care." He took a step closer. "I need to talk to you. I need to know what happened between us."

"I've told you everything there is to know. There's nothing more to say."

"Was any of it real?"

Arabella was silent for a moment. Her gaze scurried along

the ground as if she was searching for the right words. "Yes, it was. I never lied to you, everything I told you was true. But I've had feelings for Caym for a long time. I never thought I had a chance with him."

Every word caused his chest to ache, but he had to hear more. "Go on."

"When he confessed his love for me, I knew that I owed it to him — to us — to try. I'm sorry you were caught in the middle of that. I never meant for it to happen."

The expression she wore was not indicative of a person who was joyful. Her grave demeanor suggested she was anything but. "Then why don't you seem happy, Ari?"

Silence fell. Perhaps she was lost for words this time. Still, she managed to find some. "I do care about you, and seeing you like this...seeing you *at all* is difficult for me. Do you have any idea how guilty I feel?"

"Is that all?"

"Isn't that enough?" Her voice broke as she lifted her gaze. "Please, Robin, if you truly love me, you have to let me go. This can't go on. If you keep coming here, Caym will kill you. I can't have your death on my conscience."

Brow furrowed, he took a step back. If it was true that he was the reason for the look of sorrow on her features, he needed to maintain distance. The thought that he made the person he loved most in this world miserable to the core stole the very breath from his lungs.

How could he be so selfish?

"Forgive me, Arabella. I...I don't know what to say."

Despite her pleas, Robin couldn't help but think of every word she'd said before his death; how adamant she had been that there had been nothing between her and Caym. The only reason he drew breath was because of King Rydon's insistence that Arabella could not live happily without him. Was that only on account of her guilt for feeling responsible for his death?

If Arabella insisted that her king was a man of his word, why had he lied about *this*?

Raising a hand to his forehead, he closed his eyes in an attempt to silence the conflicting thoughts swirling around his troubled mind.

The next thing he heard was the voice of Galen, and when he raised his chin, Arabella was nowhere to be found. Robin did not answer the man's angry taunts.

"Who the hell do you think you are?" Galen's hand rested on the hilt of the sword at his hip. "Do you have any idea the trouble you're causing? What you're doing to Ari?" The longer Robin was silent, the angrier Galen became. "She told you to leave her alone. How many times will it take before you listen?"

He took a deep breath and decided it was best not to ignore Ari's friend. Robin couldn't blame him for being protective. "I love her. If I don't fight for her, then what kind of man does that make me?"

"A decent one!" The man's grip tightened on his sword as if to give the impression he could use it at any given moment. "Frankly, this is just pathetic. Be a man, grow up, and move on! She wants nothing to do with you, so stay the hell away from her."

As much as he wanted to, he wasn't sure he could do that. He felt compelled to be near her. But Galen was probably right, he was being an idiot. Of course he should listen to Ari, she meant every word she said. So why couldn't he promise to stay away from her?

"I know that you think I'm beneath her, but she did choose me once. She had faith in me then. Doesn't that count for something?"

"No. You're not worthy of her. Judging by the way you're

handling the situation, you never were, and you never will be. Any decent man would take Ari at her word and leave it at that. You're not even *half* the man she deserves."

Robin opened his mouth to speak, but what would he say to that? He couldn't argue that Galen was wrong. Knowing his actions were hurting Arabella, his immediate response should have been to apologize and leave, never to return. And yet, his reaction was to stay and fight.

In a way, he could understand why Queen Roanna forbade romantic relations for soldiers. He felt as though he was losing his mind. This was not the man he wanted to be.

He thought loving Arabella had made him a better man, but now it seemed that loving her made him a worse one. Or could it be that death was to blame for his untoward behavior?

"I have to find a way to say goodbye, when I'm ready. You can't force me to do that."

He didn't want to agitate Galen any further, so he left it at that and walked away.

Robin needed to get his priorities in order. This was wrong, it was *so* wrong. What was he becoming? A man without honor? He didn't know who he was if he didn't have that, at least.

Though he'd never been one to sing his own praises, Robin always thought himself to be a man of decency.

When did all of that change? When had he become all the things that Galen accused him of being?

With each gallop of Shadow's hooves bringing them closer to his half-built home, he considered his options.

Robin needed to say goodbye, somehow, in his own way. He needed to put his past, and the woman he'd thought to be his future, behind him.

Robin stood in front of his house. He was picking it apart, critiquing his own work. He had built things before, but never a house, and though he was quite certain he was the only person who would live in it, the imperfections still bothered him.

Before he had the chance to second-guess himself and tear the house down, he heard the sound of excited young women behind him.

He smiled when he saw Primrose and Bryony approach. "Is my new home to receive a royal blessing?"

"Something like that!" Bry threw her arms around him. "How are you, dear Robin?"

"I'll be better as soon as I know my roof doesn't leak."

Prim placed her hands on her hips. "That's not what she meant and you know it. How are things going with Arabella?"

Robin clicked his tongue to seem nonchalant about the situation, although his heart was shattered. "Not well, I'm afraid."

Bry's smile faded. "Oh, I'm so sorry. We never should have encouraged you, this is all our fault."

"No, it isn't," he assured them. "I'm a grown man. I knew what I was getting myself into. I should thank you both for believing in me."

"We always will." Prim nodded. "You can count on us, Robin. We'll always be here for you, no matter what happens."

He didn't want them to say such things and commit to being by his side forever. The idea of the two of them seeing him at his worst caused the ache in his chest to grow. If they ever learned what he'd done, the hurt in their eyes would be too much to bear.

They put so much trust in him, and he'd betrayed that trust. Someday, they would know; someday, he would have to tell them. He couldn't live a lie forever.

For now, he wanted to keep them as they were, untouched by whatever grief he could spare them.

"Do you want to come inside?" he asked.

They accepted the offer and he took them into his humble home. There was a kitchen, a sitting area with a fire place, and a staircase which led to a loft; he could put a bed and a chair near the window.

As simple as it was, they seemed impressed that he'd built it with his own two hands.

"Robin," Prim spoke hesitantly. "Will you let us do something for you?"

"Are you going to offer decorating advice?" He smiled. "I know it's not much. If you don't think it'll last through its first storm, you can tell me."

"Oh no, it's not that." Bry giggled. "It's lovely. Truly, it is. We just want to do something nice for you. Will you let us furnish your new home?"

Robin's first instinct was to decline. He didn't deserve their kindness. They wouldn't offer it if they knew that he'd agreed to work for the enemy in exchange for his life. "You don't have to do that. I have earnings saved. I didn't spend much of it."

"We want to," Prim spoke softly. "Please let us do this for you. We want to help. This is the first time we're able to be of some use to you."

"Don't say that, Prim. You both have given me more than you'll ever know."

"And you have been our dearest friend," Bry said in a tearful voice. "You're the closest thing we have to a brother. Let us repay you, won't you?"

"Alright." Robin pulled a handkerchief from his vest and held it out to her. "If it will stop you from being upset, I'll accept your gracious offer."

"Excellent!" Taking the handkerchief, she wiped her eyes with it and then smiled. "I'll retrieve the wagon."

Robin blinked rapidly. "You mean you brought the furniture without knowing my answer?"

"We knew you couldn't say no," Prim responded. "And we wouldn't leave until you agreed."

"Why am I not surprised?" he said with a laugh.

❧❦

FOR THREE DAYS, HE WAITED FOR SIGNS OF LIFE, FOR movement, for a sound. There was no sign of activity within the walls. Why wasn't it active? Shouldn't Arabella be outside, enjoying the fresh air? Shouldn't Caym accompany her on adventurous travels?

He didn't understand it. Happy people didn't hide in their homes. Did they really deem him such a threat?

It couldn't be that they were afraid, that they were intimidated by him. Caym already killed him once; he had that power and he could do it again. King Rydon's magic could be outmatched.

He wasn't surprised to see Galen appear from the gate. The man looked positively livid and Robin had expected nothing less.

"Can't you leave well enough alone?" Galen shouted as he drew closer.

"I've come to say goodbye," he replied. "I just need to see her once more."

"I told you what would happen if you bothered Ari again. I don't make empty threats."

Robin walked past Galen, gaze peering over the gate. He noticed someone in the second story of the manor. There was a lit window where he could clearly see a woman's silhouette. It had to be Arabella.

"I'm going to listen to you now," he spoke loud enough for the entire household to hear. "I'm going to heed your friend's words. But this is the last time I'll come for you." His breath was heavy, hands shaking as he took a step back.

This was his last attempt to communicate with her. Whatever happened tonight would be their final interaction. He didn't know if he could bear never seeing her face again — keeping his distance was akin to ripping his heart from his chest — but he had to do this for both their sakes.

The emotional blow was far worse than the one he'd been struck with at his time of death. Nothing could ever wound him as badly as Arabella's sudden departure from his life.

"I know you're unhappy," he called out. "I can see it in your eyes. I remember how you looked at me, and that's not the way you look now. But I can't keep doing this." Robin took a deep breath and closed his eyes. "The memory of us will be kept safely in my mind for as long as I live. So, do what you will. It was more real to me than anything else I've experienced in my entire life, even if it was all a game to *you*."

When Robin turned from the manor and walked back to the gate, he was almost certain Galen would cut him down. He had that look in his eye.

Before Arabella's stout protector could act, a striking woman with long, black hair and emerald green eyes stepped between them. She placed a hand on Galen's shoulder. "Not now. I know you're angry, but it's unlike you to hurt an unarmed man. You need to calm yourself."

She then turned to Robin and offered him her palm. "Will you come with me?"

He thought it was better to leave with her than stay with Galen, so he accepted it. She led him to a nearby pub and they sat at a corner table where they could have privacy.

It took him a few minutes to find his voice. "Why did you

whisk me away? Were you trying to protect Arabella and Galen?"

"No, I was protecting *you*." The beauty smiled and poured him a drink. "I like meeting new people and making friends. The opportunity doesn't present itself often, you see. I have to act quickly when it does."

"How do you know Arabella and Galen?"

"Arabella is my friend. And Galen is...well, he's more than that. Nothing official yet, but someday. I hope."

Robin raised his brow before taking a swig from his cup. "It's difficult to visualize him in a relationship."

"I know he's a bit rough around the edges. But once you get to know him, he's quite wonderful."

He had yet to see a stable side to the man, although he had to admit they hadn't met under the most pleasant of circumstances. "I doubt I'll ever know. He hates me."

"It's not you. Arabella is his oldest friend, and when she's in pain, it infuriates him."

Robin bowed his head in shame. "I never meant to cause her pain, but I was too caught up in my own to consider hers."

"I heard about what happened to you, and I'm sorry. That's why I think we'll work well together. I'm broken, and I daresay you are as well. I think if enough broken people are together, they might find a way to be fixed. It was for purely selfish reasons that I dragged you off, I assure you."

This woman had a way with words. There was such warmth in her eyes, it made him believe her to be sincere. "And here I thought you just wanted me to leave Ari and Galen alone."

She sighed softly. "You're quite unhappy. I don't like to see others unhappy. Seeing Ari isn't doing you any good, and trying to get her attention agitates Galen. And since Galen comes home to me, I would prefer him in a better mood."

Robin chuckled and shook his head. "Understood. You may rest assured; I'm not going back there. This was the last time."

"I can't begin to imagine what you're going through. I know it can't be easy. I whisked you away because you look like you could use a friend."

She wasn't wrong about that. With his secrets driving Trystan further away, perhaps it would be wise to make connections in Iros. Sooner or later, his own kingdom would attempt to banish him or worse, and King Rydon's land would be his only sanctuary. "How does one go about making friends?"

"Like this," she said with a grin. "I'm a princess, so making friends doesn't come easily. I could always use another. More-over, ones I can trust. I think a friendship could be mutually beneficial."

Another princess? They seemed to flock to him. What on earth would another princess want to do with *him*? He had to wonder what they saw in him. "I don't think Galen would like that."

She folded her arms and spoke in a matter-of-fact tone. "He does not, nor will he ever, have a say in who I spend my time with. Besides, the more our friendship blossoms, the more you'll be around, and he'll have to get to know you and see that you're not as bad as he thinks you are. And I hope *you* won't think so badly of *him*."

"I don't think badly of Galen...or Arabella, for that matter. So much about this situation is new to me. Every-thing, in fact."

"Yes, it seems you are in a unique position. I've never met anyone who's been resurrected. But you don't have to be alone." The woman placed a hand over his. "So, what do you say? Friends?"

"Only if you tell me your name."

"My name is Princess Elora Regan of Ekos." With that same twinkle in her eye, she extended her hand. "But my friends call me El."

Robin chuckled and shook her hand. "It's lovely to meet you, El."

He had never been to Ekos, but if their princess was anything to judge them by, they must have been a fair kingdom indeed to have such a kind ruler.

"May I ask why you are so far from home?"

For a moment, the sparkle in her eye seemed dull. It shined again when she smiled. "That is a tale for another day."

HE HAD BEEN TO THE MARKETPLACE BEFORE, BUT IT SEEMED foreign to him now. Retirement made him see the world in a new light. He took time to notice the smallest things that he hadn't bothered to properly appreciate before. It also meant that he noticed everything; the good *and* the bad.

Robin felt uncommonly anxious around so many people and was glad his new friend was there to accompany him.

"What kind of food do you like?" El asked.

"Uh..." He was distracted by a particularly loud seller. "Anything, really. I was raised never to complain."

El furrowed her brow. "Well, I'm not your mother. Are there things you don't enjoy eating?"

Robin chuckled. It wasn't his mother who had taught him that. "Creatures from the sea. Anything else is perfectly adequate."

She stopped at every food stand that she saw; collecting fruits, vegetables, breads, and meats. "I hope you're hungry. I tend to make enough food to feed a small army."

"Is it because you often feed Galen's friends?"

"Partly. I'm used to feeding my friends, their friends, and friends of friends... I know a lot of people."

"With you being royalty, I don't doubt that."

Elora was an old soul. She moved and spoke with such regality, such grace. Her voice was calming and any emotion she showed was subtle. They were alike that way. El must have been taught to conceal her emotions because of her status. Robin had been taught to feel numb; to desensitize himself from the world around him. It was easier that way since soldiers killed for a living.

"What is it like for you?" Robin asked. "I've spent time with Primrose and Bryony. They're so full of life, and optimistic. They see the best in everyone. What's it like for a princess from Ekos?"

There it was, that small smile that concealed a grander story. There was something in Elora's gaze that seemed aloof, as if her mind was elsewhere. "It's dangerous for me. There are more evil people in this world than I care to acknowledge. A few of them have set their gazes on me from time to time. That's why I was sent here to Iros. I'm safer here, for the time being."

Robin recognized that tone in her voice. She had suffered at the hands of others. "I assume that is how you met Galen."

"Oh, yes. He found me in my greatest hour of need. Rescued me, in fact." Her smile was genuine this time as she spoke of her love. "I don't know what I'd do without him. Or my friends. They mean the world to me. Galen makes me feel whole again." She eyed him for a moment as if she was hesitant to bring up the subject. "What broke *you*? Was it Arabella?"

Hand flexing at his side, Robin shook his head. "No, I was troubled before I met her. The last time I remember being loved was when I was a boy. To have that feeling again, and then to be told it wasn't real—" His lips pursed, steps heavy as they made their way out of the market. "Or that it *was* real and then to lose it...was devastating."

"I'm sorry." She reached out and touched his shoulder. "Will you tell me about your childhood someday? I'd like to know more about you."

"I've never told anyone," he spoke with a shrug. "I suppose I will. One day."

They trudged back to Elora's home. It was cozy; nicer and certainly larger than Robin's humble abode. It was furnished in things that Robin couldn't afford, yet it didn't feel like too much. It looked like a home, and far less impressive than one might expect to find a princess living in.

Robin prepared the fruit and vegetables while El prepared the meat. He was nervous about tonight; he could only guess what Galen might say.

"Are you sure this is a good idea?" he asked quietly.

"Of course I am. Do you doubt my infinite wisdom?"

"No...well, maybe. He hates me, El. You can't deny it, we both know it's true. I don't want him to think I'm invading his life."

"Don't you worry. He'll get used to it. One day you two will be the best of friends, just wait and see."

Robin laughed and shook his head. "Wouldn't that be something?"

Galen entered, and he didn't look surprised, so he must have been informed of Robin's visit. His gaze was narrowed, upper lip stiff, but he was silent as he greeted Elora with a kiss.

He offered to help, keeping his voice low so Robin could barely hear him. Then Galen waited at the table with a stack of papers.

He looked over them until dinner was served, and then he tucked them out of sight.

"So, what do you think of the place?" El asked as she

passed Robin a salad.

Robin would rather not have spoken. It was silly to wish to avoid making his presence apparent when he was seated beside them, but he wanted to annoy Galen as little as possible. After all, Galen had nearly drawn his sword the last time they'd seen each other. "It's lovely, Elora. It puts my house to shame."

"Oh, don't say that. I'm sure your house is beautiful." El waved her hand, gesturing to the walls of the dining room. "Galen built this before I was around, but I gave it a woman's touch once I got here."

"You did a wonderful job. Perhaps I'll hire you to fix up *my* place."

Galen grunted at that suggestion, though he didn't say anything.

"Do you have any other friends?" Elora ignored her significant other and carried on with the conversation. "I don't mean to put you on the spot, I was just curious."

"I do have a few. I've known my friend Trystan since I was a boy. He's older and always looked after me. Primrose and Bryony are the only other people I spend time with."

Galen set down his fork and stared at Robin. "You know the princesses?"

Robin met his gaze. It was the first thing he'd said all evening, and Robin was hesitant to respond. "Yes, for a few years now. I thwarted a plot to kidnap them and they've considered me their own personal Knight ever since. They're the closest thing I have to a family."

"I've never met them." Galen shrugged and returned his attention to his supper. "I wonder what they see in you."

By the sudden wince, it was clear El had kicked Galen under the table.

Robin resisted the urge to smile while focusing on his own plate. "It's alright. I wonder that every day."

CHAPTER 8

Robin didn't know what to expect. He had been waiting for this moment, and also dreading it. It was because of this man that he still drew breath, and it was because of this man that he lived with regret.

He would never have made the deal if he'd known what was going to happen. He thought that by living, he was helping Arabella. It seemed that she had found her happiness just fine without him. Now he was betraying his closest friends with nothing to show for it. His reasons for doing so no longer existed.

"Don't look so glum," King Rydon said as he handed Robin a goblet. "Are you enjoying your life?"

"So, you don't know?" He found that hard to believe. He wondered if the king knew all along, and had used his love for Arabella against him. "Arabella left me. She *doesn't* need me. She's not bound for a life of misery and doom. You lied to me."

King Rydon paused as if he were contemplating something. Then he shrugged and gave a small chuckle. "How was

I to know? Love is a fickle thing. It changes direction like the wind."

Robin rolled his eyes. "What do you want from me? There are some things my conscience won't allow; some things I'm not willing to do under any circumstances. If you ask me to kill my friends—"

Rydon scoffed and waved his hand in the air. "Stop being so dramatic. Daloran is not the only kingdom that Iros is at war with, you know. I have my eye on other realms."

Robin didn't pay much attention to Iros's other enemies. Daloran, his own country, was the only one he cared about. "So, what do you want me to do?"

"There is a land called Aryn I need you to conquer. It's filled with the lushest forests and most vibrant greenery you can imagine. Your friends will be nowhere near this fight, I assure you. They're far too busy with Iros, and I do believe one war is enough for your queen, whereas I can handle a few more."

Robin was uneasy. Relieved his friends wouldn't be there, that he wouldn't have to fight against them, but it didn't dissolve his apprehension. This would always weigh heavily on his mind. "Why can't your men conquer Aryn themselves? I'm curious. Why do you need *me?*"

Rydon tried to offer Robin food this time. He declined. "I only have so many captains. They can't all be good ones. As I said, I'm invading more than just Daloran. Do you have any idea how hard good men are to come by?"

"Luckily, no."

"Well, don't fret yourself to death, dear boy. I won't ask you to fight against your own people unless it's absolutely necessary."

Robin hoped that day would never come. The reassurance did ease some of the tension in his body. "Thank you for that."

Rydon smiled. "I'm not as soulless as some claim, you know. I like you. I admire your courage."

Robin furrowed his brow. "What courage? What have I done that's so brave? My actions prove otherwise."

"Hmm." The king scrunched his nose. "I know all about Galen. He called you pathetic, and a coward, am I right?"

He tilted his head curiously. "How did you know that?"

"I'm keeping an eye on you. It's for your benefit. People who come back from the dead have been known to develop... damage, we'll call it. Emotional as well as physical."

"Can't imagine why." Taking a step back, he rubbed his forehead. "Galen wasn't wrong. I *was* desperate. I *am*."

"So, what? You think that makes you a despicable person? I've seen cowardly, pathetic people. Don't be so hard on yourself. If I see a dark change in you, I'll be the first to tell you." Rydon poured himself a drink, again offering a goblet to Robin, who again declined. "You're of little use to me if you're corrupted. I need someone brave and loyal. You had a few bad days, it happens. If that was you at your worst, I'll count myself lucky."

"You don't think what I did is desperate *or* pathetic?"

"Unless someone has been in your position, they shouldn't judge you. Unless they've been in your place, they have no idea what you're feeling, or what the appropriate reaction is."

He hoped the symptoms of his resurrection would subside. It would take time, especially with the emotional reality of losing the woman he loved, but he had to learn to live with it. "Thank you. That makes me feel slightly better. Though, I don't think this feeling of emptiness will ever cease."

Rydon's tone changed when he spoke this time; it was low and soft, almost wistful. "The feeling of a lost love never does, my friend." He seemed to regain his senses because he cleared his throat, which deepened his voice. "Now go win me that kingdom. It'll take time to claim the entire land, but I have faith in you. I know you will accomplish great things."

As Robin tucked the last of his necessities into the back of his wagon, he saw Elora dismount her horse. She couldn't have picked a worse time.

"Where are you headed?" she asked.

"I'm off to look for work," he answered. "I have to figure out a way to pay for the rest of my life; I need to do *something*. I just don't know what it is yet, which is why I'm leaving for a few weeks."

El paused as she eyed him suspiciously. "This doesn't have anything to do with our dinner the other evening, does it?"

Robin chuckled. "No, I promise you. I really do have to work."

She must have believed him because she sighed with relief, and then smiled. "Well, then, have a safe trip."

Robin hated lying to her, even if it was only lying by omission. Elora was becoming a true friend and he wished he could tell her everything roaming through his mind. This journey would be a long one; too much time to be left alone with his thoughts.

Perhaps his new friend could put his mind at ease.

"Can I ask you something?"

"Of course," she said with a nod.

"If Galen had left you for another woman, would you have behaved the way I did?"

Her gaze wandered over him before it fell. "With our history, after what we've been through...if Galen told me he was in love with someone else, yes. Without a doubt, I would fight for him. I would need to understand what happened. And I would have to see it to believe it."

Robin felt like a fool for requiring validation, but it weighed heavily on him. To Trystan's credit, he'd been correct about the weight crushing him. It was all becoming too much to bear, and it was far from over. He had to find ways to cope.

"Thank you, El."

She smiled and placed her hand on his shoulder. "Don't worry about what Galen said. He doesn't know you. He only knows that you upset his friend. Don't judge yourself too harshly based upon the misguided opinion of others."

"I wasn't like this before, you know. Self-doubt was present, but not to the extent that it is now." He shook his head. "I don't know what happened. I don't recognize who I am. Ari did change me, for the better, I thought. And then I changed again. I don't know if dying did that or if it was Ari's abandonment."

"They were both traumatic events. They would change *anyone*, Robin." To his surprise, Elora wrapped her arms around him. "I'm glad that you trust me enough to confide in me."

"Thank you for becoming my friend. I've been alone for most of my life. I don't want to be alone anymore." His voice broke and he cleared his throat to steady it. "I want to focus on the things I do have rather than what I don't. If you hadn't pulled me aside that day, I don't know if I would have come to that same realization." He gave her a gentle squeeze and then held her at arm's length. "Arabella was the only person who gave me a chance. She got to know me, and she loved me for who I was. I was afraid that no one would ever take a chance on me again, but *you* did. I don't know how to repay you for that."

Elora's eyes filled with tears. "I'm honored to be your friend. You don't owe me anything, though I'd be delighted to have the pleasure of your company."

He suspected that she could relate to his woes, to some

extent. It was clear that Galen made her happy by the way she spoke about him, but there was still a great sadness in her eyes. It was similar to the sadness that Arabella's eyes held. It was the look of those who had suffered greatly.

"I've felt alone too," El confessed. "Galen leaves so often, and I've had to spend so much time alone. I've gotten used to it, but I can't say I like it. I think you and I needed each other. We both needed a friend and we found one another at the right time."

Robin nodded in agreement. He didn't know where he would be without her. Passed out drunk in some tavern, or sobbing hopelessly on his floor. El's friendship gave him something to look forward to; something to cherish. "I'll see you again when I return. I shouldn't be long, three weeks at the most."

ROBIN WIPED THE SWEAT FROM HIS BROW. THE TOWN WAS in flames against his orders. Rydon's men were blood thirsty. Much like their king, they desired to feel all-powerful. The soldiers he'd been fortunate to serve with had never developed a bloodlust. Every day he spent with Rydon's chosen fighters made him regret the deal they struck more and more.

It was infuriating that he was supposed to be in charge, but they wouldn't listen to him. It begged the question — what was he doing there?

His goal was to complete the task as soon as possible, but he wanted to limit the collateral damage. This village would never recover from the destruction they had caused. First they had ruined these people's lives by slaughtering a majority of their men, and now they had taken away their homes too.

Words could not describe how angry Robin was with the

situation, and, more importantly, Rydon's men. This was a matter that needed to be discussed.

He climbed to the highest point on a hill overlooking the town; its people gathered down below with Rydon's men surrounding them.

Robin closed his eyes briefly to gather his thoughts, and to ask whatever higher being there may be to forgive him for this day. "I hereby claim this village in the name of King Rydon of Iros!"

The soldiers roared with pride and raised their swords. Robin looked down at them with nothing but disdain. He wished he could offer the townspeople some words of comfort, but he didn't want to bother them. He had done enough; nothing he said would be welcomed.

He returned to solid ground and made his way toward the town's entrance. That was where they had set up camp.

Hoping to find solace in his tent, he was surprised at first to see the king waiting for him, and then he reminded himself that the royal had magic. He could appear or disappear whenever and wherever he wished.

"Well done, Captain," Rydon said with a smile.

Robin shook his head. "I don't want congratulations. Your men are savages. I told them to spare as many as they could, to not harm anyone unless they had to defend their lives. But they killed senselessly."

"Hmmm." Rydon pursed his lips. He rolled back and forth on his heels for a moment, and then crossed his hands over his stomach. "I will speak with them. It won't happen again. I trust you to act upon my will, and if they won't follow your command to the letter, they'll get what's coming to them."

"I'm not condoning their execution, I just want as little blood spilled as possible."

"Very well. You have my permission to return home for

now. But eventually, I do want the entire kingdom conquered."

"I understand that." He didn't, not really, nor did he agree with it. Robin understood he didn't have a choice, that it was his duty to follow King Rydon's orders. "And I hope you know that I plan to do that with as little bloodshed as possible. I'd prefer it if there was none at all."

"I know," Rydon chuckled. "And I don't care how you do it, spare lives at your heart's content. Just make sure the deed is done. That's all I care about."

MUCH LIKE A KING, ROBIN HAD PREFERRED NOT TO ENGAGE in the battle. He wasn't far from the action — he watched and would have stepped in had it been necessary. But King Rydon's soldiers knew what they were doing, and the royal was aware that he didn't want innocent blood on his hands.

To his relief, they followed his orders this time. Homes were burning, the streets were a mess, and the soldiers had taken control of whatever shops and stables were accessible, but no one had been killed. Although they'd ravaged the area, Robin thought it was an improvement compared to what they'd taken from the last village.

The townspeople were herded like cattle to one of the few places that hadn't been damaged: the church. Religion had never meant anything to him, but he hoped the villagers found comfort there; or as much as they could, given the situation.

It didn't lessen the guilt in the pit of his stomach. These people had lost not only their homes, but their livelihood. He wondered what they would do now; if Rydon would claim them as prisoners or demand that they work for him. Robin knew first hand that those things were practically the same.

It seemed that the two rulers he was required to serve had those similarities; they cared about power and acquiring as much land as possible, but what about the people? Without them, there would be no kingdoms to conquer, and no lands to make them so valuable.

His gaze wandered over their frightened faces, wondering how he could help them without violating Rydon's orders.

Getting the attention of a man near the church door, he lowered his voice. "See to it that they are fed. And give them blankets, please."

The soldier gave him a strange look, as if no one had ever issued such an order before, let alone with politeness.

Another soldier cleared his throat as he approached. "Will that be all, Captain?"

The word took some getting used to, even now. It was difficult to remember his position from one day to the next when he was required to play so many parts. "Has someone claimed the village in the name of the king?"

The man raised his brow before gesturing in the direction of the only hill in town. "There it stands."

He nodded, looking over the flag secured on the cliff before turning back to the soldier. "Very well. I want volunteers to guard the church until King Rydon arrives. And they are not to be harmed." Though he still had doubts that his word would be taken seriously, he knew King Rydon respected his decisions. Robin hoped to change the way the king conducted business, but looking at these victims of circumstance made him doubt his ability in that, above *all* things. "What will happen to them?"

"Since they're alive, this mission isn't considered a success. The reason for conquering kingdoms is to ensure that there are less people to take up arms against the king."

He didn't like the soldier's tone, but he appeared to be younger than Robin, and was likely ignorant. "Do you truly believe that so many innocents should die to satisfy a king's need for power?"

"Well, aren't you the hypocrite?" the man scoffed. "You were a soldier for Daloran. How is this any different?"

"Queen Roanna isn't without fault. However, there is a vast difference between fighting to gain power and fighting to defend your country. The royals I have served before now never wanted or needed more than they had. King Rydon is displacing thousands of people for his own amusement so he can have more land, and be considered more powerful."

If he hadn't been so well-liked by the king, the statement would have been viewed as treasonous. He wondered if the others would report it back to Rydon. It didn't cause him much concern because the king was well aware of his stance.

"Meanwhile, innocent people are suffering," he said gruffly, gesturing to those inside in the church.

The soldier glanced at the building, though his expression did not change. Yet another man without a care for his fellow human being. "Don't get too high and mighty, *Captain*. You are contributing to their suffering now."

ROBIN GAVE A SMALL BOW AS RYDON ENTERED THE ROOM. The dining table was set for two, but Robin was making it a point not to sit down.

"There's my favorite commander."

"Please don't call me that."

"Oh, my apologies. Should I call you my *least* favorite?" Rydon chuckled and sat at the head of the table. "Wouldn't want to make the others jealous, eh?"

"That's not what I..." The king motioned for him to sit, but he shook his head. "Your Majesty, I would rather get this over with quickly."

Rydon rolled his eyes and sighed before helping himself to the food on his plate. "Have it your way. Straight to business it is." The look on his face hinted that he was disappointed, but he said nothing and continued eating his meal alone. "You are to continue with Aryn and conquer the last few villages."

"And what will I be expected to do after that?"

"Nothing." Rydon paused and looked him over. "At least, not for a while. I will have to think of another use for you."

While he didn't like the sound of that, it could always be worse. He counted himself momentarily lucky. "Very well. Good day, Your Majesty."

"Robin," the king said quickly, "Wait a moment. I want to speak to you."

"What about?"

"To praise your tactics."

Robin furrowed his brow. He still saw himself as Rydon's prisoner, and being praised felt strange. "Whatever for?"

"You've changed how my army takes a town," he spoke in between bites. "It never occurred to me that sparing villagers might be beneficial."

The words were troubling to hear, even though he had already known them as fact. It was painful that someone of power could think of people that way, but it was to be expected. "In my humble opinion, it is better to be respected than feared."

Rydon's expression indicated that he was mulling it over. "I always thought you could not have one without the other."

Remaining at the king's side was not ideal. This was not the future he had anticipated. With every thought of wanting to be out from underneath the king's heel picking at an already tormented mind, Robin recognized that he did have some sense of influence with Rydon. If he could change the king's mind on matters such as these, it was his moral obligation to do so.

"Fear is given easily. It makes people desperate and rebellious. Respect is far more difficult to earn, but it lasts much longer. If you are known for being merciful as well as successful, others may be more willing to work with you and *for* you. The villagers included."

Rydon placed his fork on the plate of unfinished food and settled his hands in his lap. Lips pursed, he seemed to be contemplating a response; brow scrunched in concentration. He was quiet for an extended length of time; so much so that Robin feared he'd angered the royal. And then, he spoke. "You are very wise, Robin. You are able to understand different perspectives. And you have a knack for strategy. All are rare, in my experience. Have you ever thought about a political career?"

"No, I have no place among royals."

"I beg to differ. I think your friends would too."

What friends was he referring to, the ones who were oblivious to his betrayal, or the new ones that would surely grow tired of his antics? "I'd rather not discuss my friends with you."

"So defensive!" Though he was smiling, the king scoffed and returned to his dinner. "Do you not think we could be friends someday, Robin? After all this, I mean."

How could they be? To be owned by someone else was one of the worst things he'd ever experienced aside from death. He couldn't imagine *liking* Rydon, let alone befriending him. "I don't think enemies can evolve to friends."

"You'd be surprised."

It had taken two weeks to conquer the remaining villages in Aryn. In the time between claiming each town,

Robin had made certain the people were treated properly, with mercy, and without bloodshed.

After fourteen days of little sleep, Robin was in need of rest. It had been an exhausting mission.

His eyes closed as soon as his head hit the pillow.

As he drifted off to sleep, his breathing slowed and body relaxed.

Then there was a sound emanating from the back of his tent — fabric rustling.

Sitting upright, he drew the knife from underneath his pillow. The light of the moon crept in from the opening of the tent. When he saw that it was a woman staring back at him, he lowered the weapon.

"What are you doing here?" As his gaze wandered over her, he noted that she was firmly gripping a blade. "What do you want?"

He made no attempt to defend himself as the woman rushed toward the bed and held the blade against his throat.

"I've come to kill you." There was a pause as she seemed to anticipate some reaction from him. When there was none, she huffed out a breath of frustration. "Are you not afraid of death?"

"I am. But I have already died once before, you see. And the king has made it so that I cannot die again."

The woman withdrew, though her blade was still firm in her grasp. "What are you?"

"I am a man," he spoke calmly. "But I have been touched by magic."

"Why are you invading our country?"

Lifting his chin, he looked over her again, assuming that this had something to do with the chaos in Aryn. It was a wrong that seemed impossible to make right. "I'm afraid I have no choice. I made a deal with King Rydon. I'm acting on his orders." Of course, that was no excuse for his actions, and it would do little to comfort this woman. "I *am* sorry, although I know those words may hold no meaning to you. All I can promise is safe passage to you and your family. Choose any kingdom you wish and I will guide you there personally."

It was a small gesture that would never erase the carnage in Aryn, but all he could do was offer help when he was able.

The stranger's voice trembled. "Why would you do such a thing?"

"Because..." Robin took a deep breath, trying to disguise the emotion in his own voice. He hated himself for the things Rydon had asked him to do, but he truly was a man of his word – to a fault. "Despite what I've done, I understand the gravity of my actions. And I am sincere in my apology. I know what this war must have cost you."

"And what is it costing *you*?"

"My very soul."

Sliding her blade into a sheath, the woman's gaze was downcast. "I cannot in good conscience only ask for my family's safety. It must be the entire village or none of us."

"Then it will be all of you." Robin opened his mouth and closed it again. He wanted to help her and knew someone who surely would, despite the issue it would pose for him. "Queen Roanna is fair and kind. I can take you to her kingdom myself."

Another moment of silence passed. "I don't trust you. But I don't have anything to lose."

The decision had been made. His fate was sealed. "Then it's settled. Gather your family and any other refugees who wish to join you. Leave behind any belongings you can do without. We will leave at dawn."

There would be no rest for him in any corner of the world. If he was going to bring these townspeople into Daloran, he would have to explain why, and what he'd been doing in enemy territory.

Robin could continue to lie and harbor this secret, but if there was ever a cause to give reason for the truth to come to light, it should be this one; in the name of saving others.

He wondered if Queen Roanna would be lenient with him or if she would demand his head on a pike. What would happen to his mind if his body parts were separated from one another? By some stroke of luck, he may not have to offer any explanation, although that seemed unlikely.

It was time to face the truth. Shame was something he lived with every day, and yet, he wasn't ready to meet it in the eyes of those he cared for most.

CHAPTER 9

The queen had kept him waiting in the throne room. Being well acquainted with the routine of the royal family, Robin understood he had been standing before her bejeweled seat for two hours too long. No matter what was on the ruler's schedule, she had never been so tardy to a summons she herself had called for.

Gaze scanning the rows of guards on both sides of the room, his breathing became shallower the longer he stood. Cold sweat formed under the curls on his brow. Fingers interlaced behind his back.

This was deliberate. She meant to make a spectacle of him. He had seen it done many times before when a subject had been suspected of the gravest deeds against the crown.

Taking a deep breath, his gaze wandered to the pillars made of solid rock, to the ceiling carved of stone. It was not death he feared; it was endless torment.

How much did the queen suspect? How much did she *know*?

Eyes rolling backward, he was certain that he was on the

verge of losing consciousness when the great doors opened behind him.

He was afraid that a blow would come to the back of his neck, but he lowered his gaze to the marble floor, for he dared not look her in the eye.

"Sir Robin Durand."

The title made him wince. "Yes, Your Majesty?"

"Did you think it would escape my attention that your refugees came from a village in Iros?" Her tone was shrill; it must have taken a great deal of restraint not to scream at him.

"No."

"Did you think it would escape my attention that *you* were in Iros, a country with which we are currently at war?"

He took a deep breath and exhaled slowly. "No."

"And yet, here you stand." Heels clicked on the marble floor as she approached. "Kneel before your queen and explain yourself."

Shakily getting down on one knee, his head remained bowed. "Over months of correspondence, I fell in love with a woman who I later learned to be a citizen of Iros."

"Did that not give you pause?"

"It did. However, we discussed the matter and came to the conclusion that our connection was more important." Tempted as he was to lift his chin, he was concerned that it would only fuel her fury. "Neither of us had ill intentions."

"Is she a civilian?"

"No."

"A soldier, then?"

"Not...exactly." His own words caused him to grimace. The queen did not want excuses. "She is an assassin in the League of Satari."

"So, she is employed under the order of King Rydon." Her voice, no longer shrill, boomed throughout the great hall.

"Did you ask her how many Daloranians she has slaughtered?"

"No. Nor did she ask me how many Irosians I've killed."

"How thoughtful of the two of you to make an exception for one another." A staff made contact with the marble floor, so near his face that his ears rang. "And how, pray, did you come to be under the employment of the enemy king?"

"I was murdered by...the woman's acquaintance." The guards on either side of the room did not move or speak. He could only imagine the number of people behind him, as he had not heard the doors close after the queen had entered. Yet, with so many gazes fixated on them, it was eerily quiet. "Rydon came to me while I was waiting in the suspension between life and death. Before I moved on to the afterlife, he told me the woman I loved would be miserable, that she would never know happiness unless I returned to the land of the living."

"Very noble of you to return for her sake at the expense of all else," she spoke with a graveled tone. "Continue."

"I had to agree to be a captain in his army. I am bound to him; I can only die by his hand. He promised to release me from the contract once I'd served my purpose."

"You mean when my head is on a platter and he sits on my throne."

Shaking his head, his gaze finally rose to meet hers. "He never said he would harm you or your family."

"His desire is to overthrow me. Your naivety doesn't extinguish your guilt." The queen's nostrils flared. "Where is this woman now?"

Robin refused to call her by name. If Roanna wished to seek revenge, she would have to do so without his help. "She...loves another."

"You committed treason for a love that was fleeting." Again, the staff was brought down within an inch of his face.

"And to think I had considered giving my blessing for soldiers to wed. This is the result. I was right to keep the traditions of forbidding attachments."

His childhood flashed before his eyes. Years of servitude without tenderness or care, the only compassion coming from Trystan, who had, by some miracle, taken pity on him. "Forbidding relations between human beings, whether it be emotional or physical, is cruel, Your Majesty. Do not punish others for my mistakes."

"You are very bold to presume to tell me how to rule *my* people, Mister Durand."

Already, he'd been stripped of any respective stance. *Mister*. With a word, she had made her intentions known. It was no longer in his best interest to hold his tongue. "One could argue that your reluctance to encourage natural bonding for the men in your army, who work tirelessly and without reward for their entire lives without complaint, is what led to my willingness to choose love over all else."

When the staff came down this time, it did not miss his face. With a **crack**, blood dripped from a wound on his head, the crimson liquid quickly soaking through his curls. There were audible gasps throughout the great hall, and a cry could be heard behind them.

"Spoken like the traitor you are!" Roanna's steps circled around his crumpled form. "You are a disgrace to your queen and country. Do you have anything to say before your sentencing is passed?

A wave of nausea washed over him as he rose. Wiping the stream of blood from his brow, he pulled air into his lungs, albeit not effectively. It was as though he'd forgotten how to breathe. An odd sensation, seeing as he wouldn't die from lack of oxygen.

Neither living nor dead. Neither Daloranian nor Irosian. Neither soldier nor Knight.

Tears mingled with the blood that dripped onto his cheek from the steady flow of his new wound; another addition to his collection, both physical and otherwise. At least it was a wound that would heal. He wouldn't be able to say the same for the others.

"Despite being taken forcefully from my home as a child, I have given my life to the crown." Swallowing thickly, his gaze met Roanna's. His face felt flushed and he was certain that she could see the anger in his eyes. It nearly matched the disdain in hers. "All I wanted was to be with my love. It is the *only* thing I have ever asked for."

"You gave your life for the *enemy*, not for me, nor for Daloran."

"Correction, Your Majesty. I died for her, but I gave my life to *you*."

Her fingers clutched the staff tightly, appendages first turning red from the squeeze, and then white. "Was she worth it?"

It was an unnecessary question; personal, and not pertinent to use as evidence against him. It had been asked solely for the purpose of humiliation. With nothing more to lose, he refused to give her the answer she craved. "In the short time I spent with her, I had never felt more loved or accepted. For once in my life, I knew peace for the briefest of moments. She was worth my life and so much more."

"How dare you insult me!"

She raised the staff to strike him once more, but he caught it with his fist, then released it without struggle. Gasps could be heard from behind and the guards took a collective step forward.

A visible vein protruded from the queen's temple as the staff rested at her side. "How can you call yourself a soldier? A knight? You bring shame to both titles."

"I never asked to be either of those things," he spoke softly. "And I am neither any longer."

She gave him one last glance up and down before returning to her bejeweled throne, one leg crossed over the other and chin lifted. "You are hereby banished from Daloran under pain of death. And if you cannot die, you will be subjected to endless torture. You will live in exile for the rest of your miserable existence." There was a pause and then she gestured to the doors. "You may thank my daughters for the mercy you are being granted this day."

Bottom lip trembling, his heart sank as he heard the same cry that had reached his ears earlier. They had been watching the entire display.

Out of respect for the queen, even if she was no longer his to serve, Robin gave a bow and retreated from the great hall. There was a crowd of onlookers on both sides of the room. The doors remained open and he could hear the footsteps of several guards following him.

Gaze downcast, he walked past the rows of people, some throwing rocks and others throwing food. No matter the sting of various items impacting the fabric of his shirt, he gave only a grimace.

He *was* a traitor and couldn't blame them for expressing their disgust.

Three people waited at the end of the line. None of them threw anything.

Trystan's jaw was clenched, his face a mixture of red and purple that had Robin concerned that he might combust.

Primrose's arms were wrapped around her sobbing younger sister. Bryony tried to reach for him but Primrose kept her secured.

"Do not cry for me," he whispered. "No man is worth your tears."

"How could you?" Primrose hissed, one hand around Bry's slumped shoulders while the other pet her sister's long, golden hair. "We trusted you with our lives. We called you our friend."

"There is no excuse for what I have done, and so, I will give none. All I can say is that I am deeply sorry. I never meant to hurt you…or anyone. I, mistakenly, took a chance on what I hoped would be a lifetime of happiness."

His bow to them was taken with the greatest care; his stance was lowered further and the gesture lasted longer for the princesses than it had for their mother. As much as he'd respected the queen, it was Primrose and Bryony he had bonded with.

His attempt to exit the castle was blocked by Trystan. The disappointment in his eyes was the very look that Robin had dreaded all along.

"Who *are* you?"

His bottom lip trembled, though his gaze did not falter. "I am, as I have always been, your truest friend."

"Liar," Trystan hissed through gritted teeth. "My friend is dead, of that I am certain. This shell is a poor rendition of the man I once knew."

"I never meant to hurt anyone. I am *still* your friend."

"Stop saying that!" For the first time in years, or, perhaps ever in their friendship, Robin witnessed tears build in the corners of Trystan's eyes. Whether they were tears of rage or sadness, he did not know, and was afraid to ask. "You have committed treason. You betrayed your oath, Robin."

"My oath is to serve and protect the crown and *all* those I have made promises to."

"Are you trying to justify your actions based on a technicality?"

"I became disillusioned, Trystan. But I never passed along information that could be used against our country. Arabella and I were…" His voice broke while shaking his head.

"Foolish not to think of our responsibilities, but we only wanted to be together."

"You thought with your heart and not with your head. Love clouded your judgment." A poke to Robin's un-armored chest was hard enough to leave a bruise. In fact, he was certain Trystan meant to. "I'm ashamed I ever thought of you as a brother. Or a friend. If not for the respect I have regarding the queen's punishment, I would kill you myself."

Finally, Trystan stepped aside and Robin made his way out of the castle. Shadow was outside waiting for him, although he had half a mind to let him go. He deserved better than to be attached to a traitor. Surely, Primrose or Bryony would take good care of him.

Clicking his tongue, he gave a gentle tug of the horse's reins and walked him to the stable.

"You will be safe here. I'd never forgive myself if you were hurt because of me. All it takes is one stone..." He shook his head, fingers tracing Shadow's mane. "I'm sorry to leave you, old friend. But it's dangerous to be seen with me now."

The black horse whinnied and stomped its hoof as if to protest.

"Now, now, promise me you'll be good to the princesses."

Shadow snorted and shook his head.

"Oh, don't be like that. We may see each other again. I hope that we will."

"Sir Robin?"

Furrowing his brow, he turned to view Irwing in the doorway of the stable. "You needn't address me so formally, Irwing. I'm no longer your superior."

"But that's why I've come, sir," his voice squeaked. Eyes were wide and bloodshot. "Please take me with you."

"You don't understand, Irwing. I've been found guilty of treason."

"I know!" Sniffling, he took a step forward. "You weren't

sentenced to death because of your favor with the royal family, and...and because you cannot die. She'll h-hang me, or cut off my head, I'm certain of it!"

Robin raised his hand to signal for the boy to be silent. Walking past the younger male, his gaze scanned the outside area before returning to Shadow. The boy was visibly shaking, hair slick with sweat and cheeks reddened.

"It was *you*?"

Irwing nodded slowly. "I'm so, so sorry. I didn't know that you would be killed, or that Caym would abandon me after."

Robin recalled that Rydon claimed there was another traitor at his camp. He had convinced himself it was just another mind game, and yet, there stood the traitor before him. So young that his voice was high-pitched, face free of facial hair.

Would Roanna show him the same mercy? Robin ascertained that she was not in a forgiving mood. Perhaps she could tolerate one traitor. Two would be asking too much.

Hoping for the best of the queen's qualities to shine in this matter was not worth the risk of the boy's life.

"Why did you do it?" Robin whispered.

Head lowered, shoulders slumped, he began to sob. "He promised that he would return me to my family."

"Did you think the queen would stand for that when she learned that you were returned to them?"

"I-I *wasn't* thinking. I just miss home."

How could Robin condemn him for that? He was an adult and still missed his family. There were many days when he longed to see them again. While he hadn't betrayed his country to return to them, he may as well have. He had committed treason for the chance of a *new* family with Arabella.

Hearing footsteps near the stables, he glanced toward the doorway and saw Trystan coming toward them.

"Don't say a word," he whispered to the boy. "Follow my lead and I'll take you away from here."

"Robin," came his friend's gruff voice. "What are you—"

Moving swiftly, Robin grabbed Irwing by the shoulder, spun him around to face Trystan, and held a blade to his throat. "The boy is coming with me."

Trystan's mouth fell ajar. "What good is he to you? He's practically a child, not much older than you were when I took you under my wing."

"You heard the queen. My safety isn't guaranteed. I could be apprehended at any time before I reach the border, and I'm not keen on being tortured for an eternity."

The older man's gaze wandered over them, head shaking in disbelief. "How far you have fallen. Using a boy as a shield..."

"Let us pass."

Trystan growled, gaze fixated on them. They knew each other so well that Robin understood by the glazed over look in his friend's eyes that he was livid, and contemplating his next move.

Robin would never dream of hurting the man, but was relieved when he stepped aside. He didn't have the heart to raise a sword to Trystan. While neither would be truly harmed because Robin could not die, and wouldn't lay so much as a scratch on the other, it was the symbolism of the thing.

Swords should never be drawn between friends. And the fallen knight would never cease to think of Trystan as such.

Blade falling to his side, he assisted Irwing onto the horse, and then mounted behind him.

With a nudge from his ankle and the click of his tongue, Shadow sped past Trystan, out of the stables, and down the path.

Reaching the border would take days, if not longer, especially with another person. His main concern was getting the boy to safety. If they were taken by the queen's guard, he would likely break under the pressure and seal his own fate.

❦

EYELIDS HEAVY WITH EXHAUSTION, HE SHOOK HIS HEAD TO remain awake. Irwing and Shadow had gotten rest during each stop whereas Robin had to keep watch. They were near the border, so it wouldn't be long until the boy was safe.

"What are you going to miss the most about Daloran?" Irwing asked softly.

"The beauty of the land. The peace among the trees. The quiet of the rocks." The sky was gray this morning. Birds were silent as a strong wind whistled off the boulders scattered across the acreage on either side of them. "I miss simply existing in the countryside. My family owned a farm. Our neighbors were few and far between, though everyone knew one another. There was true comradery there."

"Like it is in the army?"

"No, not quite. In the army, men are forced to be civil. In my hometown, everyone genuinely cared for one another. Being ripped from such a warm environment was... cruel. And cold. Very cold." He couldn't speak for every village in Daloran, but he would credit his town for teaching him the value of a tender heart. "Don't lose yourself, Irwing. It's easy to forget oneself in times of war. And that is the majority of our lives as soldiers. Don't let anyone take away your spirit."

A boulder etched with an arrow pointed forward and the words 'Border Ahead' seemed to pass more slowly than the others. It caused the breath to hitch in his throat. At the same time, he heard sniffling from the boy in front of him.

"Why are you being so k-kind to me, sir?"

"You don't have to call me that anymore, remember? And why shouldn't I be?"

"Because I'm the reason you died…"

Sighing heavily, he paused in the hopes of finding adequate words to still Irwing's tears. "You are not to blame for my death. The fault lies with Caym and him alone."

"So, you're not cross with me?"

"Not at all, Irwing. I, of all people, understand why you did it."

The boy's shoulders slumped. "I know how selfish it was. And that we're fortunate that we weren't all slaughtered in the night."

"You are young and we all make mistakes. Going forward, you must strive to do better."

"Do you think Rydon will reunite me with my family and allow us all to live in Iros? That is, if they miss me enough to betray their country too?"

He nodded slowly while mulling over the possibility in his mind, well aware that Irwing couldn't see the gesture. "He seems to be a fair man, by all accounts. He may help you, but…I don't know him well enough to say for certain."

Shadow stopped, his hooves stepping on the borderline. One more step would guide them to a ship that would ferry them to the Half-Point, and to another ship that would sail them to the Kingdom of Iros. In some ways, their journey had ended. In other ways, it was only beginning.

Robin clicked his tongue, gave a light tug of the reins, and encouraged his horse to continue.

"We can rest shortly, Irwing. And then you may sit behind me if you wish."

"Why is that?"

"In Daloran, we were in danger of being shot in the back. No one will do anything of the sort here. There is no jurisdiction. We're not quite at the Half-Point yet, but it's the reason

I built my home on the land between the two kingdoms. Everyone is civil and kind. It reminds me of my hometown."

There was a pause. Irwing looked over his shoulder at the older man. "You can't go back there now, can you?"

"No, I think not. The only place Roanna won't hunt me down, jurisdiction or not, is in Iros."

Irwing patted Robin's arm. "I'm glad you will be there with me. A familiar face among a sea of strangers."

It wasn't an ideal situation by any means; hardly something worth celebrating.

However, Robin understood that he had the chance to right one wrong; to be there for this boy in the same way Trystan had been there for him.

He could only hope history wouldn't repeat itself. Irwing had betrayed him once; there may come a time when he would do so again.

Robin had betrayed Trystan after over a decade of friendship.

Time would tell.

"For your sake, I hope your family will join you. Your adolescence is far from over and you will need all the support you can get."

"What if they can't? Or worse...what if they don't want to?"

"You will always have me. I will not abandon you, Irwing."

⚜

"Robin, what in the world..." Shaking her head, Elora gently wiped the dried blood that had crusted onto his forehead. "I can't believe you traveled all this way with such a wound. Look at the state of you!"

He shrugged and the sting of the bruises adorning his bare chest and back made him wince. "We needed to reach

Iros as quickly as possible. I wasn't concerned about the wound. It's not as though I could die from an infection."

"No, you'll just ask Elora to cater to your every need," Galen snarled.

Scrunching her nose, she tossed a clean cloth toward her partner. "It's not like you to kick a man when he's down."

"Depends on the man, my darling."

With a roll of her eyes, she rose from her chair and soaked the soiled cloth in a basin of water. "I'm going to make a poultice for you. Because you are my friend and I *want* to." She shot a look in Galen's direction.

"He's right, El." Robin brushed wet curls from his forehead. "You're too good to me."

"No, *you* are too good for that tyrant of a queen." She mumbled something under her breath that made Galen's eyes widen, though Robin couldn't hear. "Excuse my language."

Being none the wiser to whatever she had called Roanna, he smiled and shook his head. "This is your home, you can say whatever you like."

"Oh, that reminds me." Elora opened her cupboards and pulled herbs from several shelves. "Where are you going to live?"

"I don't know. Suppose I'll have to build again."

"You could—"

Galen growled and folded his arms. "Don't say it. *Please* don't say it."

"Whyever not?" Turning to face him, she placed both hands on her hips. "We have a perfectly good structure that he could make his own." With no further argument, Elora smiled at Robin. "There is a shed on the property. It's not much. Smaller than this, but big enough to live in. You are welcome to it."

Gaze moving from Elora to Galen, Robin nodded slowly. "I will consider it. Thank you for the kind offer."

LAURENCIA HOFFMAN

"And don't mind him." El waved her hand toward her part‐
ner. "I'll make sure he minds his manners."

KING RYDON APPEARED AS THOUGH HE DIDN'T HAVE A
care in the world. He was feasting on a plate full of food.
Robin had, once again, opted to remain standing.

The room was silent; that seemed to be their usual stance
when they didn't see eye to eye on a subject. Rydon wanted to
be friends, but Robin couldn't see past his predicament.

To the King, his banishment from Daloran was neither
here nor there. He was thrilled to have the fallen knight at his
whim, even more so now that he was trapped in Iros.

Finally, he cleared his throat and said, "I have a bone to
pick with you."

Rydon raised an eyebrow. "Just one?"

"Why did you lie to me about Arabella?"

With a scoff, Rydon set down his silverware. "I beg your
pardon?"

"I agreed to this arrangement because you told me that a
terrible fate awaited Arabella if I did not return to the land of
the living. You *lied*." That was the only reason he made the
deal in the first place. If he had known then what he knew
now, he would have chosen to remain in the afterlife. "She's
happily with another man. It's difficult to imagine she ever
truly loved me. So, I don't understand how you can pride
yourself on being a man of your word when you lied to me."

Rydon's expression changed to one of anger. Then, almost
as soon as it had appeared, it was gone. A softer look came
over his features as he picked up his fork and began to eat
again. "I'm not a liar, Robin. It's insulting of you to call me
one."

"Is something terrible going to happen to her?" Perhaps it

was simpler than that. Her happiness would surely plummet if something happened to the man she loved. Could misfortune favor her twice? As devastated as he was with the outcome, he could only feel an overwhelming sense of empathy at the thought of Arabella losing anyone she held dear, even her current lover. "Or is Caym the one in danger?"

"That is not for me to say." Rydon avoided his gaze, carefully chewing his supper between sentences. "And since you think me a liar anyway, it wouldn't matter what I said. You wouldn't believe me if I told you the truth."

"What *truth*?" Robin waited for an answer but realized he wouldn't receive one. It was beyond frustrating and he wished it didn't bother him so deeply. No matter what had happened between them, he would always be concerned with Ari's happiness. If she didn't have her happy ending, then it was all for nothing. "I wish you'd stop playing games with me."

"I don't play games." Rydon lifted his chin. He looked as though he might say something, but then thought better of it. "You will learn soon enough."

ACKNOWLEDGMENTS

Back in ye old days of Myspace, I was involved in a writing roleplay group of fantasy characters. Our characters came from places like Middle-earth and Narnia. At the time, those two worlds were immensely popular in the roleplay community!

I was a young teen when I began writing with the group. We lost touch after a couple of years. During the height of our roleplay, I remember thinking what a cool story it would make.

My roleplay group encouraged me and I began writing this book. It was challenging to take the story apart and piece it back together. I rewrote it several times over the years. It's taken me over a decade to figure out how to build my own world while somehow paying homage to the themes that made Robin's journey special to me when he was first born.

There were times when I wanted to give up because it was too difficult and I was certain people wouldn't find my fantasy world *believable*. Ironic, I know. But I did it! I finally rewrote the entire story, keeping only details and events that specifically happened to my character. His love interest, circle of friends, and enemies were entirely rewritten (for obvious reasons)!

When I learned the book would be published, I knew I wanted to acknowledge my roleplay group in some way.

AFTERWORD

So, to my old friends:

I never forgot the stories we created together, and if you read this, I hope it brings back fond memories. You welcomed me into your circle and gave me an outlet when I was most in need. To the people who helped me develop this character, encouraged my creativity, and instilled a passion for him that continues to exist all these years later, thank you.

ABOUT THE AUTHOR

Laurencia Hoffman specializes in various sub-genres of romance. Her stories often focus on the darker side of fiction, but love and survival remain the central themes throughout her work.

When she's not writing, she also enjoys playing video games with her family, listening to music, satisfying her sweet tooth, and watching films.

.

Made in the USA
Monee, IL
15 September 2021